Her Montana Cowboy
Valerie Hansen

D0311091

HARLEQUIN® LOVE INSPIRED®

Special thanks and acknowledgment to Valerie Hansen
for her contribution to the Big Sky Centennial miniseries.

Recycling programs
for this product may
not exist in your area.

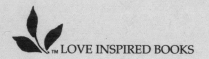

™ LOVE INSPIRED BOOKS

ISBN-13: 978-0-373-81774-0

HER MONTANA COWBOY

www.Harlequin.com

Printed in U.S.A.

He is our God and we are the people of His pasture, the flock under His care.
—*Psalms* 95:7

To my Joe, who is with me in spirit, looking over my shoulder and offering moral support as I write. He always will be.

Chapter One

The glorious day! Finally!

"Here they come!" Julie Shaw jumped up and down, clapped her hands, whistled and shouted with the rest of the spectators lining the parade route.

After months of preparation and thousands of volunteer hours, the Jasper Gulch centennial celebration was finally kicking off with their Fourth of July parade.

Proud beyond words, Julie placed her hand over her heart to honor the American flag as the mounted color guard rode beneath one of the vibrant banners spanning the street and passed the reviewing stand filled with local dignitaries. Seeing the entire two-block stretch of old-town Main Street decked out in red, white and blue, with myriad flags flying, brought tears to her eyes. What a country. What a town. And what a beautiful state Montana was.

Her eldest brother, Cord, was one of the riders chosen to carry the fluttering Stars and Stripes and open the festivities, following a short speech from their father, Mayor Jackson Shaw, and a prayer by the new pastor, Ethan Johnson.

Feeling blessed, Julie watched the passage of the various homemade floats bearing veterans, the Little League team, 4-H members and many others. Her happy heart was beating in time with the drums of the Jasper Gulch Bobcat Band as it marched by. Those kids might not have fancy, matching uniforms, but they were all dressed in their best Western wear, as was she, and their enthusiasm was contagious.

Following the float bearing Miss Jasper Gulch came a mounted group of rodeo participants, led by the clowns, who much preferred to be referred to as bullfighters. Of all the events scheduled for the six-month-long celebration, it was the rodeo Julie loved best.

Her sister, Faith, elbowed her in the ribs. "Hey, look."

"I know. I'm looking." Julie blushed and fanned herself with her straw Stetson to exaggerate her reaction. "Wow!"

"And you said there were no handsome men in Jasper Gulch."

"Not exactly. What I said was, there's nobody around here I'd consider marrying, no matter what Dad wants."

"It's the same thing."

Julie shook her head. "No, it isn't." She would have continued to spar with her older sister if her attention had not become focused on one passing cowboy in particular.

She couldn't decide what it was about the man that had caught and was holding her attention. It had simply happened. There was something so special, so compelling about him she could not tear her gaze away.

He sat comfortably in the saddle with his hat pulled low enough to shade his dark eyes. Fringes of dark hair were visible at his nape, leaving the rest of his hair to her imagination.

It would be thick and wavy, she told herself. And it would feel—

Another poke in the ribs startled Julie. She jumped.

"Whoa," Faith said, giggling. "Earth to Julie. Where was your mind just now?"

"I'm not telling." The warmth of her flushed cheeks did the talking for her and caused her sister to laugh louder. Julie tried to quiet her. "Shh. You're making a scene."

"Not me, baby sister. You should see your face. It's almost as red as your hair."

"We have auburn hair, not red," Julie countered. "I just wish I didn't blush so easily."

"Comes with our blue eyes," Faith told her. "That, and freckles, which I could do without."

"Don't be silly. You have beautiful skin."

"Speaking of beautiful, take a gander at the barrel racer your cowboy is riding with."

"He's not with…" She'd been going to finish with "anybody," until she looked back at the procession. The good-looking rodeo rider who had caught her eye did seem to be in the company of another woman. Not only that, the horses they were riding sported similar tack. They certainly looked as though they were a couple.

Nevertheless, Julie shaded her eyes with one hand and boldly studied the man. She hadn't met nearly all the rodeo contestants because many had arrived in Jasper Gulch very recently. Their normal schedule would have had them competing here for two or three days, then packing up and moving on to the next PRCA—Professional Rodeo Cowboys' Association—sanctioned rodeo. There were plenty to choose from and she was doubly thankful that so many talented contestants had opted to honor her town with their presence.

Not only that, some had agreed to remain or return for a second and third weekend. It didn't hurt that the invitational events included some of the biggest names in rodeo, plus monetary grand prizes and serious day money for the top qualifiers. That kind of reward was definitely worth vying for.

The muted *clip-clop* of hooves on the wide main street sounded soothing. If Julie had not been so keyed up, she might have been able to relax and enjoy the rest of the parade more. The sights were certainly pleasant enough—particularly *one* of them.

Suddenly deciding what to do next, she clapped her hat back on her head, turned away and started into the crowd lining the curb.

Faith grabbed her arm. "Hey! Where are you going? The parade's not over."

Exactly where *was* she going? Julie hesitated, her mouth slightly open. "I just..."

Her sister hooted as she let go. "You're going to move up so you can watch those attractive guys ride by again, aren't you?"

"Of course not." That was true if she took the question literally. It was not *guys,* plural, she wanted to study more. It was just one of them.

Yes, it was crazy, she admitted to herself. And yes, it was a tad embarrassing. At least it would have been if she'd imagined for a second that the rider had even noticed her. Cloaked in anonymity, she had no qualms about watching him pass a second time. And maybe a third.

Julie shook her head, slightly disgusted with

herself for even contemplating changing her position along the parade route. That didn't stop her, though.

She approached the corner of Main Street and Shaw Boulevard, the street named after her ancestors. Here, the marchers would turn south toward the fairgrounds and rodeo arena. This would be a perfect place to wait and watch.

It occurred to her to wonder if she would even recognize the handsome cowboy again. In an instant, she had her answer. There was no way she'd ever forget him. It was as if his image had been permanently imprinted on her mind.

"I am certifiably unbalanced," she murmured. "If Dad heard what I'm doing, he'd blow a gasket." Knowing that her father fully intended to choose her boyfriends, or at least vet them, she smiled. Wouldn't it be funny if she showed up at the picnic later on the arm of a rodeo rider?

Oh, yeah, like that's going to happen, she told herself wryly. Still, she began to work her way through the mass of bystanders lining the streets bordering the old bank building that housed city hall and the chamber of commerce. All she had to do was get close enough to peek over the heads of some children and teens standing at the very front. Being taller than Faith by a few inches had helped her see well before. This time, she aimed to put herself in an even better position.

Smiling and being as polite as possible, Julie said, "Excuse me? Please?" then "Thank you" as she wormed her way forward.

She reached her goal and looked up just as the group of riders began to arrive, found the man she was searching for and stared directly at him, never dreaming he'd pay any mind to her unjustifiable interest.

Her sharp intake of breath sounded a lot like a gasp. Her jaw dropped. The cowboy's glittering brown eyes were boldly meeting hers. She was captured as fully as if he'd dropped a lasso around her and pulled the loop tight to reel her in.

He inclined his head, touched the brim of his hat politely, smiled—and *winked.* At least she thought he did.

No, that wasn't entirely true. She dearly hoped he'd winked on purpose. *At her.*

Ryan Travers was used to encountering rodeo groupies and had learned that the best ways to discourage them were to either face the problem boldly and announce that he wasn't interested, or to avoid them entirely. In the case of this pretty admirer, he decided to adopt a wait-and-see attitude.

Besides, he thought, letting his grin widen, she was different somehow. Naive, maybe? She certainly looked it. Then again, looks could be deceiving. In a small community like Jasper Gulch the girls were likely to be… He started to think of derogatory terms, then abandoned them in favor of simply enjoying the view.

The rider beside him inclined the brim of her pink Stetson. "Heads up, Travers. You have an admirer. The one in the bright blue shirt."

"I noticed. Kinda cute, too."

"If you like sheep."

"Beg your pardon?" He knew Bobbi Jo was competitive in the arena, but he had no idea she carried that attitude over into her personal life. "What have you got against her? You don't even know her."

"Matter of fact, I met one of her brothers yesterday and he pointed her out. She was helping decorate the fairgrounds' picnic area. She actually does raise sheep."

"Here? Why?"

"Apparently for their wool. She's got some kind of internet business selling yarn or some such thing. Sounds pretty dull."

Ryan huffed. "Sounds downright suicidal to me. Sheep in cattle country? How does she get away with it?"

"It might help that her daddy is Jackson Shaw, the town mayor and owner of the largest ranch in this part of Montana. I guess he can afford to designate some of his pasture land to his little girl's sheep ranching."

"Ah, I see." Too bad, he added to himself. The

lovely young woman seemed hospitable enough, but chances were her well-to-do parents wouldn't welcome an itinerant cowboy into her life, any more than the old-time ranchers had a hundred years ago, back when Jasper Gulch was founded.

Bright sunlight peeked between the flat facades of the commercial buildings, temporarily blinding him. When he looked back for the auburn-haired sheep rancher, she had gotten lost in the sea of similar cowboy hats.

He stood in the stirrups of the barrel-racing horse he'd borrowed from Bobbi Jo's string and scanned the onlookers for a bright blue shirt. There was no sign of the young woman.

The horse instantly reacted to his change of balance, prancing as if getting ready to race into an arena and compete.

By the time Ryan got the fractious horse under control, the riders had crossed Massey Street and were on their way out of town to the fairgrounds.

What shocked him most was his clear disappointment over losing sight of the mayor's daughter. Try as he might, he could not shake the feeling that they would meet again.

Matter of fact, he assured himself, he would see that they did, one way or another.

Children on bikes decorated with red, white and blue crepe-paper streamers followed the main part of the parade, taking care to dodge the droppings the horses had left behind. Julie had recruited members of the local 4-H club to follow and clean the street. That was one of the jobs she'd volunteered for years back when she was a member, and she saw no reason to abandon a tradition that helped build character.

That notion made her smile. It was her membership in 4-H and, later, Future Farmers, which had eventually led to her current career, and she was truly grateful. Raising sheep for wool was not only lucrative, it was rewarding in emotional ways. Seeing those tiny lambs struggling to their feet for the first time was akin to watching a sunrise on a summer day. Those woolly babies were a new beginning, new life, always bringing waves of joy as well as making her feel connected to the land, to nature, in a very basic way.

The rumble of an ATV approaching behind her caused Julie to step aside. It stopped next to her and the driver tipped his battered Western hat. "Howdy, Miss Julie. Like my new camo-painted Mule?"

Seeing ninety-six-year-old Rusty Zidek traveling via anything other than a horse or his dented antique Jeep struck her funny, but she managed to keep from giggling. "Hi, Rusty. I know that thing is called a Mule but it's still a surprise to see a veteran cowhand like you behind the wheel."

"Compliments of your daddy." The grizzled old man's grin crinkled his leathery skin, lifted the corners of his bushy gray mustache and exposed one gold tooth among his others. "He made me traffic manager and gave me these wheels. Pretty spiffy, huh?"

"Absolutely. We'll need your help a lot with all the visitors in town. Parking at the fairgrounds is bound to be a nightmare."

"Not with me in charge, it ain't. I got me a bunch of retired yahoos with nothin' better to do and put 'em to work directin' traffic."

Julie chuckled. "Good for you."

"How's about a ride? Or did you bring your truck?"

"No. I hitched into town with Dad so I wouldn't add to all the extra traffic." She stepped in and settled on the bench seat next to the bony nonagenarian. "Much obliged."

"No problem, ma'am. Where to?"

"The picnic grounds, I guess."

Julie was sorely tempted to ask him to drop her near the encampment where some of the rodeo participants had grouped their trailers, but quickly thought better of it. Competition was scheduled to last for three weekends. There was no hurry finding out who anybody was.

She huffed, then glanced at Rusty, hoping he hadn't noticed. It wasn't just anybody she wanted to learn more about. It was that cowboy who had smiled and winked at her during the parade.

And the first thing she'd need to learn, she reminded herself, was whether or not he was with someone, namely the gorgeous cowgirl in the pink Stetson. If he was spoken for, Julie figured she might as well go home and card wool or rake the barn. There was no way she could hope to compete with a blonde, shapely woman who looked as if she were Miss Rodeo America, or recently had been.

Man, that was a depressing thought, she countered, disgusted for having entertained it. Either she believed her life was in God's hands or she didn't. It was that simple. And that complicated. The hardest part of trusting her faith completely was making sure she stayed out of the Lord's way instead of trying to figure out His plans and help them along.

Pastor Ethan Johnson was one of the few people in whom she had confided a tiny bit of frustration with her personal life because she could tell he understood. He should. New in town, he was basically in the same boat: single, eligible and determined not to be pushed into anything by well-meaning do-gooders.

Julie's biggest problem was with her father. He wanted all his kids married and having families, as if that would help him hang on to the spirit of Jasper Gulch that was their heritage.

She had nothing against tradition. She simply wasn't positive her dad was right about some of the notions he insisted on espousing, such as leaving the old bridge the way it was instead of improving it. For a man who had been so instrumental in putting together this six-month-long commemoration of their history, he certainly was close minded about other things.

Yeah, like who I should marry, she added with a heavy sigh. If she "accidentally" ended up in the company of Wilbur Thompson, one more time she was going to scream. Oh, Wilbur was nice enough. He was just not the man for her, no matter how successful he was or how much money he'd invested in the town via his position as bank president. No man in a three-piece suit belonged on a sheep ranch. Period.

"And I don't belong in some fancy town house, either," Julie muttered. She didn't realize she'd spoken aloud until Rusty chuckled.

"What makes you say that?"

She shrugged. "I was just thinking about Dad. I'm only twenty-four, but he acts like I'm already over the hill and keeps pushing me to marry some rich guy. If I gave in, I'd probably end up living in town and trying to be somebody I'm not. Just picturing it gives me the shivers."

"I can sure understand that, Miss Julie. You and me, we're a lot alike." He laughed raucously. "If I was fifty years younger I'd propose to you myself!"

Julie joined his amusement and patted the back of his weathered, gnarled hand as it rested on the steering wheel. "Rusty, if I were fifty years older, I'd accept."

She nearly busted up laughing when he waggled his bushy gray eyebrows at her and said, "In that case, I'd be forty-six and you'd be seventy-four. I'm afraid you'd be *way* too old for me."

Chapter Two

Ryan joined Bobbi Jo at her horse trailer, took the time to properly store her saddle and bridle, then fed and watered the horses for her before following his nose and sauntering over to the picnic grounds.

Someone had covered a bunch of long wooden tables with white paper to serve as disposable tablecloths. Centerpieces displaying tiny flags, red and blue flowers and ribbons sat on each, while a bank of serving tables held enough food for the entire town, and then some.

The aroma of barbecued burgers and hot dogs mingled with that of baked beans, making his mouth water. Cold potato salad and coleslaw finished the main course, while several men were busy in a separate area slicing watermelon and offering it to the revelers filing past the dessert table.

Not one to hang out with only rodeo contestants

the way most of his friends did, he freely mingled, chatting amiably as he filled a foam plate. Because he was concentrating on the food, Ryan failed to notice who happened to be dishing up coleslaw.

When his server's hand stopped in midmotion, he looked up—and into the widest, bluest eyes he'd seen since he'd noticed the same young woman watching the parade.

He grinned at her. "Yes."

"Um, yes what?" she asked, remaining immobile.

"Yes, I'd like some slaw and yes, I'd also like to know your name."

She would have plopped the spoonful of cabbage into his hot beans if Ryan had not hurriedly turned his plate.

"Easy, there. Don't make me spill the beans."

"What?" Her cheeks flamed. "Oh, sorry."

"Okay. Now, what's your name?"

"Julie."

"Pleased to meet you, Julie. I'm Ryan. Ryan Travers."

From behind him came a testy "Hey, quit holdin' up the line. Other folks are hungry."

Ryan nodded politely, balancing his plate on his palm and touching the brim of his hat with his free hand. "Guess I'd better move along. I'll be sittin' right over there by the watermelons, Miss Julie, in case you want to join me later."

"Aren't you going to eat with the other cowboys? Dad reserved a couple of tables for all of you."

"I'd just as soon make myself comfortable where I don't have to worry about impressing anybody. It's so crowded over there nobody will miss me."

Although she didn't comment, didn't even smile, he got the feeling she'd do her best to at least stop by before he was done eating. Why he'd invited her was almost as much a puzzle to him as her obvious personal interest. He'd chosen the life of a traveler a long time ago and, although he was no longer a rookie, he was far from ready to retire at twenty-seven. Given the ages of many of his fellow riders, he probably had ten more good years in him, provided he didn't suffer any bad injuries.

That was the main drawback with earning a living as a rodeo rider. Every time the chute opened, he stood a chance of being hurt. Maybe even crippled. Or killed. He never allowed himself to dwell on worst-case scenarios, but they lurked in the back of his mind just the same.

Which was one of the reasons he avoided romantic entanglements. That, and the conviction he didn't deserve the kind of lasting happiness he'd seen some of his buddies find along the way. There were too many dark shadows in his past, too many sins for which he'd never forgive himself, let alone share with a naive, innocent woman like Julie Shaw. Her daddy was the town mayor. That pretty much said it all.

Ryan sighed, unwrapped his plastic fork and dug into his food. Sure, it was a boost to his ego to have a pretty girl notice him, but that didn't mean he intended to take her interest seriously. He'd tell her about his rodeo career, impress her properly, then bid her goodbye the way he always did when he met someone interesting on the road.

That was one of the perks of traveling from rodeo to rodeo. Nobody expected him to hang around, so there were no hurt feelings when he left town. His life was simple. Fun. Rewarding when he won and tolerable if he happened to finish out of the money, which, thankfully, didn't happen too often.

If the time ever came when he wasn't winning regularly and building up his bank account enough to make everything worthwhile, maybe he'd hang up his spurs and invest in property where he could raise good bucking stock. Until then, he'd keep riding and choosing his venues to turn the best profit. That was one of the benefits of belonging to the PRCA. Their organization provided plenty of opportunities all over the country to compete for high stakes.

Ryan sensed a presence behind him and gave

the front brim of his Stetson a poke with one finger to raise it so he could look up more easily. It was her! *Julie.* And she was obviously planning to stay because she was balancing a laden plate of her own.

He smiled and rose as best he could in the confines of the attached bench. "Ma'am. Can I fetch you a drink? The lemonade's real good."

"Yes, please. If you don't mind."

"No problem. Just keep an eye on my food for me. I'll be back in two shakes."

"Of a lamb's tail," Julie added, blushing and averting her gaze. "I raise sheep for their wool."

"So I've heard."

Her head snapped around and she stared at him. "You have?"

"Uh-huh. Stay put. I'll be right back and you can tell me more about it."

It was all Ryan could do to keep from laughing as he turned and headed for the lemonade. Clearly, Julie was used to being disparaged for her choice of livestock. Little wonder, since she lived in cattle country. If his vested interests had been in ranching, he might feel the same. However, because he was only passing through, it made no difference what kind of damage her flock did to the grazing lands thereabouts. After all, her daddy was a cattleman as well as a local politician. Chances were, he had enough influence to keep Jasper Gulch ranchers from running her out of town on a rail.

Ryan's grin broadened as he made his way back to his table with a plastic cup of cold lemonade. Julie's story was likely to be interesting. And she was certainly easy on the eyes. This promised to be a really nice afternoon. One he was looking forward to.

If someone had asked Julie how long she'd been sitting there, talking to the fascinating rodeo cowboy, she'd have said it had only been a short time. That was why, when the PA system sounded off, inviting revelers to gather at an old wooden bandstand at the edge of the main picnic area, she was astounded. One glance at her watch confirmed that she'd lost track of time.

"Uh-oh. I'm supposed to be with my family when my father makes his speech."

"About the celebration, you mean?"

"That's part of it. There's also a time capsule buried behind the stage. It was put there during the christening of Jasper Gulch a hundred years ago and everybody's pretty excited about digging it up and seeing what's in it."

"Surely you must already know. I mean, didn't the town's founding fathers write it all down back then?"

Julie shrugged. "Beats me. I suppose they must

have, but there's no telling what happened to that record. A lot of artifacts were ruined back in the fifties when a sprinkler system in city hall malfunctioned and everything in storage molded."

"What a shame." Ryan got to his feet and began to gather up their trash. "You go join your family. I'll take care of this."

"Nonsense," she said, reaching for her plate. "I can clean up my own mess."

"I'm sure you can. But you have somewhere to go and I don't. I'm in no hurry."

"Aren't you riding today?"

"Not until after three. I have plenty of time." He patted his flat stomach. "I ate too much anyway. Need to go walk some of this off."

"You said you compete in rough-stock events, right?"

"Yup. Bareback and saddle bronc first, then bulls last, right before the fireworks."

"I'll try to be there to watch you."

"Good. Maybe your good vibes will help me win."

Pausing, she decided to speak her mind. "I don't believe in that kind of influence. Skill matters, of course, but I prefer to trust the Lord."

The expression on his face told her more than she wanted to know, particularly when he said, "Afraid I can't agree. It's just as likely that we're all responsible for our own fate." He swept his arm in an arc as soon as he'd dropped their refuse in a trash barrel. "Look at all this. Do you honestly believe a divine Creator is keeping track?"

Hands fisted on her hips, she faced him. "Yes. I do."

It distressed her to see him shaking his head. "Not me. I used to think it was a possibility once, but I've learned different."

"That is so sad."

"More than you know," Ryan mumbled.

He had not been facing her fully when he'd spoken, but she could still make out the words. For all his bravado and flirting and apparent sense of self-worth, he was as lost as one of her lambs in a snowstorm. Her heart went out to him.

Lost is exactly what he is, she concluded.

So treat him kindly and demonstrate God's love followed as clearly as if her pastor had been standing there, preaching right to her.

Was that why she'd met Ryan Travers? Was she supposed to minister to him? Or was she simply so enamored of this particular man that she was inventing reasons to hang around him? If her former, elderly minister, Pastor Peters, was still around, she could ask him without embarrassment. The new clergyman, Ethan Johnson, was another matter. Not that she didn't trust him to keep the few confidences she'd already shared.

She was simply shy about baring her most intimate thoughts to a person she hardly knew.

Nevertheless, Julie reasoned, there was plenty of scripture that explained how to approach a skeptic. And since Ryan Travers sounded disillusioned more than unbelieving, she already had a foundation upon which she could build.

Assured, she hurried to join her father and the local dignitaries, who were about to unearth the time capsule. Guesses about what it contained had been floating around town for months. It would be interesting to see how many of them were right. Plus, her dad had invited the press, not to mention a TV crew from Bozeman that was doing a live remote broadcast of the unearthing of the capsule before moving on to cover the rodeo action. This was the biggest party Jasper Gulch had ever hosted, and it promised to make the news all across Montana.

The old bandstand had been repaired and repainted so many times its floor rippled and the stairs leading up to the main stage had depressions worn in the center of each step. Overcome with nostalgia, Julie envisioned a community orchestra playing a waltz and finely dressed couples from just after the turn of the twentieth century dancing on the grass where groups of people now milled around in anticipation.

Julie joined her family in a row of folding chairs onstage. Everybody was there. Her mother, Nadine, was straightening Jackson Shaw's string tie. All three of her brothers, Cord, Austin and Adam, were grouped together, chatting privately while waiting for the speeches to begin.

Faith waved gaily and patted an empty chair. "Over here. I saved you a seat."

Trying to appear unruffled, Julie fought to catch her breath. "Thanks. I was afraid I'd be late."

"Oh? Where were you? As if I didn't know."

Warmth crept up her neck. Julie knew her cheeks had to be flaming. "I was eating."

"I saw. How did you manage to displace the barrel racer? She was with the rest of the riders, the way your new friend was supposed to be."

"I guess Ryan is more of a loner," Julie said with what she hoped was a nonchalant shrug.

"Didn't look that alone to me. You two were sure having a long conversation. So spill. What did you learn about him?"

"Um, not a lot. He's been riding professionally since he was a teenager and specializes in the three rough-stock events."

"Where does he come from and where does he live when he's not traveling? Who's his family? Are his parents living? What's his ranking so far this year?"

Julie's jaw dropped. "I didn't ask."

"Then what in the world did you find to talk about?"

"Sheep, mostly."

Faith rolled her eyes. "Well, you can probably cross that cowboy off your list. I can't imagine anybody being as enamored of fleeces as you are."

"He seemed interested."

Cocking her head to gesture without drawing undue attention, Faith indicated a portly, well-dressed businessman mounting the steps to join the people already assembled on the bandstand. "Wilbur acts that way, too, when he's trying to impress you."

"That's only because he gave up on you. I thought Dad was going to explode when you turned the guy down flat."

"I do have my moments of lucidity." Faith giggled. "Poor guy. I know he tries."

"Who? Dad or Wilbur?" Julie gave the banker the once-over. He had pudgy cheeks to match his expanding girth and so little hair that he'd combed it in a style that made it stick to his forehead as if he thought bystanders would be fooled into thinking he had more hair.

"Definitely poor Wilbur," Faith said.

"I know. He reminds me of that English teacher

we used to have in high school. The one with the nervous tic."

Faith chuckled. "I remember. And you're right. Mr. Thompson does kind of resemble him."

"You do realize, don't you, that if I keep turning down Wilbur's social invitations, Dad may decide he's the right man for you after all? You are older."

"Perish the thought. I suppose he'll make a great husband for somebody, but he's not my type."

"My sentiments exactly." Julie brightened. "Hey, maybe you should reconsider. Wilbur might build you a music room if you married him."

"I'd rather play on a city sidewalk and let people throw coins into my violin case than marry somebody for money. As far as I'm concerned, my music is my life."

"A violin won't keep your feet warm in the winter," Julie teased.

"I suppose you think I should get an Australian shepherd like yours."

"It beats accepting a man our father has picked out for us. Besides, you could do worse. *Cowboy Dan* is a great dog."

Faith was smiling and shaking her head. "You always were a sucker for animals, Julie. You've brought home critters ever since you were little. It's no wonder you like to hang out with sheep and sheepdogs."

"They accept me just as I am," Julie countered.

"And they never, ever try to guilt me into dating and marriage. What's not to love about that?"

All Faith said was "Amen, sister," leaving Julie smiling behind her hand and hoping their father didn't notice her lack of decorum as he began his speech.

Ryan chose to meander around the fairgrounds, getting his bearings and greeting old friends from prior rodeos before heading for the bandstand. The mayor's oratory was not high on his bucket list, nor was he willing to stand around wasting time when he could be sizing up the livestock on which he made his living.

Only one thing drew him to the bandstand. Julie had told him she'd be there, making a command performance, and he wanted to see her again.

Why?

Good question, he asked himself and answered. She wasn't like most of the women he met in his travels. Matter of fact, she was so different, so open and honest, she'd made quite an impression on his jaded attitude about buckle bunnies. That term for the female groupies who frequented rodeos made him smile. He always kept his clothing pure Western and shunned the ornate silver and gold buckles he'd accumulated as prizes, rather than wear them as badges of honor. Every ride was another chance to prove himself to the judges and the fans. It wasn't necessary to brag about his prowess by donning an enormous gaudy oval emblem at his waist.

"Besides," Ryan said aloud, "broncs and bulls don't know the difference or care how many events I've won. They just want to buck me off."

Which was why he should be back at the stock pens taking another look at the caliber of animals he'd draw from later today. And he'd go soon, he promised himself.

Right now, the focus of the crowd seemed to be shifting. People onstage were getting to their feet, and it looked as if Julie was about to accompany the mayor and his delegation to wherever their ancestors had buried the time capsule.

As Ryan observed the area, he noted a black-and-white poster displayed on an easel. It was a fuzzy blowup of an old, damaged sepia photograph. Five men in dark suits, cowboy boots and bowler hats were leaning on shovels and grinning at the camera. Behind them was the same bandstand that still stood, but the nearby trees were a lot smaller. He judged the wooden box in the foreground to be about two foot square, give or take. At least they knew what the time capsule looked like.

Curious, he followed the procession to a shady area behind the back of the old bandstand. There, the ground was dry and had been trampled by so many feet it would have been impossible to tell exactly where the current digging was going to take place if there had not been a cement marker.

He eased to the side, placed his back against a wooden wall flanking the rear of the stage, folded his arms and waited. He'd abandoned any notion of finding Julie in that milling crowd when he'd seen how difficult it was going to be. Therefore, he'd set himself up so she could locate him. Assuming she wanted to.

Ryan's pulse jumped. Apparently, she did.

A smile began to lift the corners of his mouth and had spread into a wide grin by the time she managed to work her way to him. "Hi," he drawled. "I wondered where you'd gone after you came off the stage."

"I'm supposed to be up front with Dad and the others for a photo op. I'm playing hooky."

"Something tells me you don't like being in the spotlight."

"You're right. I only do it to please my folks, and then not always. I'm here today because I respect my father and want to support him. And Jasper Gulch."

"You've lived here all your life." It wasn't a question.

"Yes. And I plan to stay. It's more than home, it's where I have my business and where my family is." She smiled wistfully. "What about you? Where does your family live?"

"My mother's in Bozeman."

"Wonderful. Then you can visit her while you're in the neighborhood."

"I suppose." He deliberately changed the subject and took her elbow. "Come on. Let's go try to find a place where we can see the time capsule when they bring it up."

"Okay."

Julie gave no sign she was surprised by his abrupt action. Good. He didn't like to talk about his past or what was left of his family. Growing up with an absent father and then losing his only brother in that terrible crash had been bad enough without having to explain to an outsider.

Ryan's jaw clenched. Even visiting his mother briefly was hard. Seeing her again rekindled all the feelings of loss and anger and guilt he'd borne for so long. He'd never attempt to describe all that to anybody else, of course. Just feeling it himself was painful.

A stump amidst the grove of remaining trees caught Ryan's attention and he pointed. "That way. Next to that bunch of reporters."

Julie smiled up at him. "I see what you mean. Think we'll both fit on the stump?"

"No, but I'll make sure you don't fall off," he promised.

Taking her hand, he helped her step up onto the

rough, weathered surface and steadied her. "Can you see now?"

"Yes! They've moved the marker that was on top and have dug almost down to the concrete vault. As soon as they pry up the lid and get the actual box out, the committee will carry it back to the stage and open it in front of everybody."

Watching her pretty face, Ryan noticed her smile fading and a scowl taking the place of her earlier elation. Her hold tightened. She glanced at him, clearly troubled.

"What is it? What's the matter?" he asked.

Julie was acting as if she was in shock. Flashes from cameras blinded everyone.

The TV crew had surged forward and one of them was shoving a microphone on a boom at the dignitaries. Someone was counting backward, "Three, two, one…" preparing to broadcast live.

"We're here in Jasper Gulch for the unearthing of their time capsule and the mayor has just opened the vault!" a female reporter shouted into her microphone as the crowd began to rumble with an undercurrent of disbelief and astonishment. "Get a shot of that hole," the woman yelled aside to her camera crew before returning to her broadcast. "They've just opened the sealed vault, ladies and gentlemen. It's empty!"

Julie saw the reporter gesturing as the spectators pushed in around the site.

She held out her hands to Ryan and he helped her safely step down from the stump.

"What could you see?" he asked.

"It's gone," Julie told him in a hoarse whisper. "The vault is empty. The capsule's been stolen!"

Chapter Three

Julie lagged behind with Ryan as the crowd dispersed, following her father and the rest of the centennial committee around to the front of the bandstand. She wanted to look at the empty concrete vault herself, as if needing proof that the time capsule was really missing.

"There's no way anybody could find clues here now," Ryan observed. "This dirt has been trampled by too many boots." He was crouching next to the open hole while curious onlookers slowly passed by, whispering, pointing and conjecturing.

"I know." Julie was more than disappointed. She was crushed. "What a shame. Opening the capsule was one of our main events. I can't imagine who would have bothered it."

Dusting off his hands, Ryan straightened. "One thing you might want to ask yourself is if it was taken recently or pilfered a long time ago."

"I'd never thought of wondering why the dirt looked freshly disturbed. I just assumed it was loose because somebody had prepared the site for easier digging when the TV cameras were rolling."

"That's possible," he replied with an arch of his dark eyebrows. "It seems likely that the theft occurred after everybody was reminded that the box existed. The old-timers who buried it in the first place knew what was inside. Folks today probably didn't, unless that rickety old guy I saw you with earlier today was alive back then."

His lazy smile warmed her and temporarily alleviated some of the tension. Julie began to smile again. "Rusty Zidek. He's a fixture around Jasper Gulch. I'll do you a favor and not tell him you just said he was rickety. He's proud of being in his nineties."

"Perfectly understandable," Ryan replied. "If I were his age and still that spry, I'd brag about it, too."

She grew pensive. "You know, even if the original records of the burial of that box have been lost, it's possible Rusty remembers rumors from when he was a boy. It might be worth asking him. I'll suggest it to Dad in case he hasn't already thought of it."

"Okay." Ryan checked his watch. "I hate to miss any of this excitement, but time's getting short. I'd better head over to the arena and see to my bare-back riggin'."

"Where do you fall in the schedule?" Julie asked, fully intending to watch him ride every chance she got, as promised.

"I'm fourth up in the bareback lineup, near the last in saddle bronc and the same in bull riding." He grinned. "Guess the officials are saving the best for last."

"Good to see a humble cowboy for a change," Julie quipped.

"Hey, confidence is necessary if I intend to win," Ryan countered. "You can't be unsure of yourself and expect to stick eight seconds on a bucker, especially if it's an eighteen-hundred-pound bull."

She allowed herself to assess him for a few seconds, then said, "The bigger ones are probably a better fit for a guy as tall as you are. I imagine those small bulls are a lot harder to ride."

"Especially if they're slab sided," Ryan explained. "It's like being a contestant in mutton busting when you're a kid."

"That reminds me," Julie said. "I have to see to the sheep I brought to town for that event. The children always look forward to pretending they're big ol' tough cowboys. It's adorable to watch. I just hope my sheep don't have nervous breakdowns."

"What little I know about sheep, it wouldn't

take much. They aren't the most intelligent critters in the barn."

She huffed and planted her fists on her hips. "Well, they're smart enough to stay away from wild horses and angry, bucking bulls."

Laughing, he touched the brim of his Stetson. "You've got a point there, ma'am." As he backed away, he gave her a parting grin that made her toes tingle inside her boots.

"I'll pray for you. Okay?" she said.

"Whatever." Turning on his heel, he left her without further comment.

As Julie watched him go, she pondered their previous conversations. Most riders she knew were pretty reliant on the good Lord to watch over them, and many could cite instances when they'd felt God's protection, even if they'd been injured.

Apparently Ryan Travers was a long way from embracing her kind of faith. Julie sighed, disheartened by that conclusion. It was not her habit to try to change folks when they were happy being whoever they'd decided they were, but in Ryan's case she'd make an exception. Denying God's loving kindness and infinite power was bad enough. Doing so when you regularly risked your life was much, much worse.

Julie nodded and smiled at the accurate assessment. And he thought *sheep* were clueless.

* * *

For the first time in longer than Ryan could recall, he was having trouble keeping his mind on his work. He couldn't have cared less about the missing time capsule; it was pretty Julie Shaw who occupied his thoughts.

"That's not good," he muttered as he stood on a metal rung of the narrow bucking chute and tightened the cinch on the surcingle that was the main part of his bareback rigging. This rangy pinto mare wasn't called Widowmaker for nothing. He knew she followed a pattern around the ring that was not only erratic, she tended to change her tactics if the rider on her back got the least little bit off center.

Off center was exactly what he was, too, Ryan concluded, except his problem was mental. He could not only picture Julie Shaw as if she were standing right there next to the chute gates, he could imagine her light, uplifting laughter.

Actually, he realized with a start, that *was* what he was hearing. He started to glance over his shoulder, intending to scan the nearby crowd and, hopefully, locate her.

"Clock's ticking, Travers," the chute boss grumbled. "You gonna ride that horse or just look at her?"

Rather than answer with words, Ryan stepped across the top of the chute, wedged one leather-gloved hand into the narrow, rawhide handhold that was his only lifeline while aboard the bronc, folded back his fancy chaps and settled himself as gently as possible.

The horse's skin twitched. Her ears laid flat. She was gathering herself beneath him, knowing it was nearly time.

Ryan raised his free hand over his head and leaned way back so his spurs would fall at the point of the horse's shoulder when she took her first jump. Then he nodded to the gate man.

The latch clicked.

The mare leaped.

Ryan held tight, determined to keep his feet in the proper position for a legal mark-out. If he let either heel pull away or drop too low before the mare's front feet landed that first time, he'd be disqualified. Then it wouldn't matter how well he rode or how hard this horse bucked. He wouldn't get a score. Period.

Since half the points awarded were for the rider's performance and half were for the horse's, he also wanted her to do well, meaning he had to not only keep his balance, he had to make the proper countermoves to get the most out of this ride. Eight seconds didn't seem like very long until you had your fingers wedged into a grip sticky with resin, the horse's hind legs were flying so high you were being flung against her spine and the whiplash made it feel as if your head was fixin' to part company with the rest of you.

Ryan didn't attempt to do anything but ride until he heard the horn blast announcing his success. Then he straightened as best he could and worked his fingers loose with his free hand while pickup men maneuvered their running mounts close enough to help him dismount.

One of the men flicked the flank strap and it dropped away, stopping the mare from trying to kick it loose.

Ryan grabbed the other rider's arm and released his glove while the mare traveled on without them.

"Thanks, man," Ryan said, dropping to the ground next to the pickup horse and getting his balance well enough to scoop up his bent Stetson and dust it off.

"Watch it. Here she comes again," a wrangler warned. "She'd as soon run you down as look at you."

It was immediately clear to Ryan that the man was right. The rangy brown-and-white horse had missed seeing the exit gate on her first pass and was coming around again. Fast and furious.

He leaped up on the nearest fence. To his delight, Julie Shaw and a few others he recognized from before were watching. They had parked a flatbed farm truck near the fence beside the grandstand and were watching from secure perches in its bed.

Julie had both arms raised and was still cheering so wildly she almost knocked her hat off. "Woo-hoo! Good ride, cowboy!"

Ryan's "Thanks" was swallowed up in the overall din from the rodeo fans. Clearly, Julie wasn't the only spectator who had been favorably impressed.

A loudspeaker announced his score as eighty-six and a quarter.

Julie cupped her hands around her mouth and shouted, "You were robbed!" which made him smile even more broadly.

He knew he should immediately report to the area behind the strip chutes and pick up his rigging. And he would. In a few minutes. As soon as he'd spoken to his newest fan.

The soles of his feet prickled in his boots as he jumped off the outside of the fence and reached behind to loosen the thigh buckles on his chaps.

"I'll take any decent score I can get," he said, wanting to reassure her that he wasn't upset about her hometown event. "When I'm going for all-around in rough stock, every completed ride is a good one."

She climbed down to join him and lightly touched his arm before facing the people she was with. "Ryan Travers, this is my sister, Faith. You probably noticed her at the parade. And this is Hannah Douglas, one of my very best friends. The adorable twins are hers. The boy is Corey and the girl is Chrissy."

Ryan tipped his hat. "My pleasure. I think I met Mrs. Douglas at city hall when I checked in as a competitor."

"That's right," the dark-haired, dark-eyed young woman said. She laughed lightly. "At least I think we met. I've seen so many strange cowboys lately they're all starting to look alike."

"Not to Julie, they don't," Faith chimed in.

Ryan almost laughed aloud when he saw Julie shoot a look of disdain at her sister. She was even cuter when she was blushing, and she was certainly pink enough now. So much so that the contrast of her freckles had almost vanished.

"Want to come with me to claim my rigging?" Ryan asked, assuming everyone would know which woman he was asking.

When all three answered in the affirmative, his jaw dropped—until the other two began to laugh and he realized he'd been the brunt of their inside joke.

"No way," Julie announced boldly. "This one is all mine." And with that, she took Ryan's arm and urged him to walk away with her.

He was unsure how to best respond until she abruptly released her hold and apologized. "Sorry.

I'm not usually so pushy. My sister knows how to get my goat, but Hannah doesn't often help her."

"It must be nice to be so close."

"Yes. You don't have siblings?"

Although he tried to mask his feelings, there was apparently enough poignancy in his expression to cause her smile to fade when he said, "No. Not anymore."

She didn't ask further questions, nor did she offer unasked-for advice. She simply slipped her hand through the crook of his elbow again and tightened her grip.

If Ryan had been asked to interpret her actions at that moment, he probably would have said she was offering moral support. That was certainly the impression he was getting. And, like it or not, her presence was helping him handle the guilt and sorrow he still carried in regard to losing his big brother, Kirk.

Pushing aside those disturbing memories with Herculean effort, Ryan placed his other hand over Julie's and kept walking. If he could have done so without attracting undue attention, he would have kept her by his side indefinitely.

There was something very special about Julie Shaw. Something he could not explain. Something intrinsic that emanated from her as if she were the personification of acceptance. And of love.

Caught unaware by that random thought, Ryan

almost pulled away from her. Yet, he didn't. And the why and wherefore of that choice troubled him deeply.

Julie yearned to urge Ryan to confide in her more. To let her help heal his obvious emotional pain. If he would tell her about his problems, she might know better how to pray for him.

"As if God needs *my* input," she muttered as she left him checking his bronc-riding gear for his next event and headed back to rejoin Faith and Hannah. True, scripture urged praying without ceasing, yet she also knew there were references to God knowing what His children needed before they even asked. In the case of that spiritual truth, and others, Julie didn't mind admitting she was confused.

Besides, she thought, climbing back aboard the truck bed with her friends and adjusting her straw Western hat, Ryan had made it clear that he did not share her Christian beliefs. That was even sadder than the way he was apparently mishandling his grief. Life without faith had to be much harder, losses more difficult to accept.

It was always sad when a person suffered. It was doubly devastating to see someone trying to cope without the Savior to lean on. Temporal friends could offer only so much comfort. Jesus would be there to help no matter what the circumstances, but only if He was invited.

This could be a pride problem, she reasoned, particularly in the case of a man like Ryan Travers. He was used to doing things his way, relying on his own strength. And, unfortunately, it looked as if he had failed to overcome whatever trauma had led to his no longer having any siblings. Oh, he probably thought he'd gotten over the loss, but he hadn't. Not even close. Was that what drove him to stay on the road most of the year? Julie wondered. Perhaps. And perhaps he didn't even realize why he was so restless.

Or maybe all this is a figment of my imagination because I don't want to admit he's happy traveling all the time, she countered. Just because she was a homebody and content to have deep, strong roots didn't mean that a person who preferred to move around had to be unhappy.

She sighed and released her angst. It didn't matter why Ryan competed all over the country. He was who and what he wanted to be, regardless of his motivation.

Meaning they were totally incompatible, she concluded in spite of mental arguments to the contrary. Yes, he was appealing. And yes, she really liked him. But getting too attached to him would be a big, big mistake. One she was determined not to make.

Chapter Four

Ryan had not intended to hang around behind the scenes when the mutton busting was introduced as part of the afternoon's entertainment. He simply had little else to occupy him while the bareback horses were removed and saddle broncs loaded into the holding pens directly behind the chutes. Stock contractors had their own wranglers and treated those horses better than a lot of folks treated their kin, meaning they didn't want them touched by anybody else.

He got himself a bottle of cold water and drank it as he ambled over to the place where a passel of youngsters was gathered. A twenty-something man he recognized from the mayor's entourage was instructing the kids about safety, so Ryan figured he was probably one of Julie's brothers.

Some of the little boys and girls looked overconfident, while others seemed scared to death.

It was those children who tugged at Ryan's heart and caused him to edge closer.

He spotted one boy who seemed far too small and timid to be competing, and crouched down to speak with him. "Hi, there. Where's your mama? Does she know you're planning to try to ride a sheep?"

Although his lower lip was trembling, the little boy stuck out his chin and ignored the question.

"A grown-up has to fill out paperwork for you, buddy. You can't enter without your mama or daddy being here."

Tears welled in the child's eyes as he looked around. "Mama's here."

"Where?"

"I—I lost her."

Straightening, Ryan offered his hand. "Okay. Why don't you come with me and I'll introduce you to the lady who owns the sheep while we wait around for your mother to come looking for you. Then, in a few years when you're older, maybe you'll be all ready to ride like the bigger kids."

"Uh-uh. Can't go with strangers. Mama said."

"And your mama is absolutely right," Ryan assured him. "But since she's bound to look for you where she saw you last, I think it would be okay to hang around and talk to the sheep lady for a bit. Her name is Julie. See? She's right over there. The pretty one with the dark red hair and the straw Stetson."

Smiling, he followed the little boy's tentative steps as they skirted the group of excited children and approached Julie. The moment she looked up, he tipped his hat and eyed the boy. "My friend and I were wondering if we could maybe give you a hand. He wants to ride, but his mama got herself lost, so she isn't here to sign for him. Would you mind if he petted your sheep?"

The grin Julie returned rested on him first, widened, then switched to settle on the uneasy child. "Of course not. They're pretty tame, particularly around me. I'm afraid I've made pets of them."

"Hey, as long as you're raising them for their wool, no problem, right?" Ryan offered.

"Right." Julie held out an arm. "Would you like to come in here with me or do you want to stay outside with your cowboy friend?"

The boy seemed to be considering carefully before he reached for Ryan's hand and grasped it firmly. "Stay here." His upturned face searched Ryan's. "Okay, mister?"

"Fine with me."

Ryan swallowed past a lump in his throat. He wasn't sure what touched him more, the boy's trust or the gentle expression on Julie's face when she looked at them standing there together. Here he was, a tough-as-nails guy who faced fifteen-hundred-pound-plus belligerent farm animals, and he'd been reduced almost to tears by a small boy and a pretty woman. If his old friends could see him now, they'd probably laugh their spurs off.

And he didn't care, he suddenly realized. At this time, in this situation, he was so at peace, so filled with joy, he truly didn't care what anybody else thought.

That's not entirely true, Ryan mused. He did care about one person. And she was bestowing the loveliest, most warm and wonderful smile he'd ever had the pleasure to receive.

If he'd been the romantic type, he might even have said it made his heart sing.

Julie saw plenty of happy families all around her, yet had eyes only for the stalwart cowboy and the trusting little boy. There was something endearing about them, not that she hadn't seen plenty of fathers and sons together before.

She turned back to her tasks with the sheep, but her mind continued to dwell on Ryan. Perhaps the sight of him befriending the boy seemed so wonderful because he had told her he was close to no one, had no family other than his mother, whom he rarely saw. It was almost as if Julie was being given a glimpse of the kind of father he could someday become.

"Are those girls or boys?" Ryan's young friend asked.

"These are all girls. Mama sheep are called ewes," Julie replied. "I brought these to the rodeo because they're so friendly."

"I know horses can live twenty years or more," Ryan said. "How old are these animals?"

Julie chuckled. "Be careful you don't hurt their feelings. They might take offense if they knew you'd called them old."

"Sorry. It's hard to tell."

"It can be unless you're used to judging sheep. These are about eight. As long as I have the room and plenty of feed, they'll live out their natural lives in my flock."

"Not a very practical approach to ranching," the cowboy said.

"Yes and no. Business is good and they still produce fine wool. Sales have really taken off since I updated my website. I've had to hire more help for lambing and shearing."

Whatever happened, Julie was determined to keep her hands on every aspect of Warm and Fuzzy. The name of her business went back to her days as a youngster in 4-H, and it always made her smile. So did being in the company of gentle ewes and their lambs. Adult rams were another story. She never turned her back on them, even in the off-season.

"I can't figure out the look of that wool," Ryan said. "It's almost silky."

"That's because I specialize in Leicester Long-wools."

"Lesters? Like in Lester Flatt and Earl Scruggs, the bluegrass pickers?"

Julie chuckled. "It's pronounced Lester but spelled *L-e-i-c-e-s-t-e-r.* They're rare but have amazing fleeces."

"They certainly do. Not that I've paid a lot of attention before. I guess you can tell I'm used to hanging around horses and cattle."

The young man helping her offered his hand to Ryan. "Me, too, but I got roped into this. I'm Adam, Little Bo Peep's brother."

The men shook hands.

"You're forgiven—but Adam *isn't,*" Julie said with a mock scowl. She shooed him back to work and returned to her interrupted conversation with Ryan.

"The Jasper Gulch Chamber of Commerce and Event Committee thanks you and all your fellow competitors for being here," Julie said formally.

"I'd rather you thanked me personally," Ryan said "Will you be free tonight during the fire-works show?"

"I'd planned to watch with my family. There are a lot of us, and we usually make a party out of it." Hesitating, she finally added, "If you want to join us, you'll be most welcome."

"Thanks. Where will you be?"

"On the old bridge over Beaver Creek. It's one of the reasons we decided to hold such a long celebration instead of just remembering the town's actual founding date. We're trying to raise money to repair the picturesque sites like that bridge and encourage tourism. Being so close to Yellowstone Park, we think we'll have a fair chance of success, particularly if we can add a scenic route to the option of driving through Jasper Gulch instead of going around it on the highway."

"I guess that makes sense for folks who have the time to just look at scenery. I'm always in a hurry or driving at night to make the next competition."

Julie straightened and shook her head as she gazed at him and said, "That's sad."

"Not to me, it isn't. I happen to like my life on the road."

What could she do but smile? "Then more power to you. There are too many people who never decide what they want to do or who they want to be. One day they wake up and realize it's too late for them."

She checked her watch. "Speaking of late, I need to get these ewes lined out so the kids can start."

"Go right ahead. We'll just watch. Right, buddy?"

The child tugged on his hand. "There's my mama!"

"Then you'd better go tell her where you are so she doesn't worry."

"Yeah!"

Julie paused as soon as she'd guided the first two ewes into the narrow passageway to the make-shift chutes the kids were using. "That was sweet of you."

"What was?"

"Looking after that little boy until his mother found him. She must have been worried sick."

Ryan shrugged. "Maybe. I didn't do it for her. She should have kept better track of him."

"I'm sure she tried."

"Maybe."

Watching his changing expressions, Julie wondered why the mention of a mother's care and concern seemed to bother him so much. Was that why he'd been so noncommittal when she'd asked if he intended to visit his own mother? Perhaps. Then again, maybe he was simply the kind of adult who looked out for the welfare of children.

And damsels in distress, she added silently,

stifling a telling grin. There was no way she'd ever qualify as a damsel, in distress or otherwise. Given her ability to take care of herself beautifully, as well as running a ranching and internet business, she knew she wasn't the type of woman who brought out a man's protective instincts.

"Well, thanks anyway, on behalf of Jasper Gulch," Julie said pleasantly. "This is a safe little town when we're not entertaining so many visitors. Dad hired extra sheriff's men to help the regular deputy, Cal Calloway, patrol during our special events. Truth to tell, a few men in uniform would never be able to handle all the problems that might arise if we didn't look after one another the way we always do."

"I'm sure your old friend Rusty would be glad to strap on a six-shooter and help," Ryan teased.

He was trying to lighten the mood, Julie decided. And to distract her from the way his persona had hardened in defense of the child. This cowboy was a complex person, one who chose to keep his true emotions in check and present himself as a carefree drifter. He was not. She might hardly know him, but she could tell that already.

The true puzzle was not what he did for a living, it was *why*. Lots of young men rode well and could have competed the way Ryan did, yet most chose to stay home and use their skills on family ranches. This talented rider insisted he was proud of having no roots, of being totally free.

But he was not free, she concluded. Far from it. He was bearing a burden in his heart that she had only glimpsed. In the days to come, while the rodeo continued, she planned to find out more. To try to understand his motivation for breaking old ties and not forming new ones.

And in the meantime, she would do the only thing she could. She would pray for him and wait for the Lord's guidance.

Ryan stood at the fence for a few minutes to watch the kids hanging on to the ewes' fleece while the fractious sheep raced across the arena. There was no riding gear other than helmets for each child to wear, so they had to grab fists full of wool and just hope their feet didn't slide too far to one side. Most ended up in the dirt in one or two seconds and half were crying when they were helped to stand, despite the applause from onlookers.

He'd never had the privilege of competing like this. If his big brother hadn't taken him under his wing and taught him to ride, he might never have discovered how good he was or how much he loved rodeo. That was before Kirk had gotten involved with a bad crowd and started leaving him home to go out drinking; before he'd climbed behind the wheel of a car and died in a wreck blamed on drunk driving.

I should have told on him. Only I didn't, did I? Ryan mused. Not that it would have made any difference. Their mother was always too busy working to pay much attention to her sons.

Ryan would probably have dropped out of high school if it had not been for the rodeo team and its coach. By the time he graduated, he was already winning local prizes. After that, it was just a matter of getting his seasoning on the road and finding his niche. He'd traveled with a couple of buddies until he'd saved up enough to buy a nice truck and strike out on his own. Now he preferred to go it alone. It was better that way. There were no scheduling conflicts to resolve and nobody minded if he won steadily, outearned his rivals and kept growing his bank account.

The first saddle broncs were already waiting in the chutes by the time he worked his way around the arena. Mutton busting was over and the winners were proudly waving their blue ribbons while the clown-face-painted bullfighters held them up to the accolades of the crowd.

Ryan spotted Bobbi Jo in the distance and raised a hand to wave. She responded with a smile and started toward him. She wasn't his type, but she was a faithful friend, one who was always willing to loan him one of her spare horses if he needed a mount for the grand entry or, like today, for a parade. The fact that she had a small fortune invested in her horses made her generosity even more out of the ordinary.

"Need help pinning your number on?" she asked.

"No, I've got it. I took the vest off and did it myself."

"*Humph.* I'd have thought you'd recruit your new girlfriend to do the honors."

"She's not my girlfriend. I barely know her."

"Give it a week or so," the pretty barrel racer said. "Then tell me you aren't interested in her."

"Not gonna happen," Ryan insisted. "Julie's roots are deep here. There's no way she'd pull up stakes and follow me all over the country."

"Why not? I do."

"You're not here because I am," Ryan said flatly. "You're here because this is the best prize money for time spent and you know it." He purposely changed the subject. "I understand your practice runs were very good."

"Not as good as they'll have to be to beat the others. That older woman from Oklahoma is a racing fool. And her horse is part Arabian, so he never gets tired."

"You'll do fine," Ryan assured her. "Just don't knock over a barrel and pick up penalties."

"Oh, sure. Like all you have to do is keep from getting bucked off and you'll win, too."

"It's a start." He chuckled. "I'll try to watch your run while they're getting the bulls moved up."

"Thanks."

As he left his friend, Ryan recalled how Julie had promised to pray for his success. It must be nice to believe in God so strongly that she could rely on the power of prayer rather than skill.

He had no such delusions. He was in the competition because he was good at what he did. That was all there was to it. And until he was either incapacitated or got too old to compete well, he was going to keep going. Keep traveling. Keep striving to be the best in the business and take home the biggest purses. Lack of interest in roping might keep him from ever winning all-around titles like Ty Murray had, but his riding would keep him in the spotlight, hopefully for years to come.

There was nothing more he could ask. Nothing else he wanted out of life, at least for the present.

In the back of his mind, a thought that was barely there asked, *Really?*

Chapter Five

If the afternoon had been a bit cooler, Julie might have left her ewes at the rodeo grounds until the end of the day. The humidity was low, but once the daytime temps reached into the mid-eighties she decided to ask her youngest brother, Adam, to haul them home for her.

She rode along. "So what did you think when the time capsule turned up missing?"

He shrugged. "Beats me. Dad was sure steamed."

"At least he kept his cool and got the crowd to move away from the site. I don't suppose the sheriff's officers we had patrolling the grounds came prepared to investigate a crime like that."

"Not when Cal and the extra deputies were hired just for crowd control," Adam replied. "There's a forensics team coming in from Bozeman, but I don't expect them to find anything."

"I agree." Julie was nodding thoughtfully.

"Ryan asked if the theft might have occurred a long time ago."

"Ryan? The guy I met by the sheep?"

"Yes. He's one of the rough-stock cowboys. I met him this morning and we seemed to hit it off really well."

Her brother chuckled. "I want to be there when Dad finds out you're interested in a rodeo rider."

"Why, because you plan to defend my right to pick my own husband?" She had to laugh at the irony. "Give me a break. You have enough trouble keeping the girls at bay with him and Mom shoving them at you. The way I see it, since you, Cord and Austin are all older than Faith and I, you guys should get married and settle down first."

"Life doesn't work that way, baby sister. When it's time for me to find a wife, I fully expect her to fall into my lap, not show up because our folks have been matchmaking."

"Well said." Julie relaxed, leaned back and sighed. If she allowed herself to accept her brother's reasoning, she might actually start to believe she'd met Ryan Travers because he was the one for her. Was that possible?

Not rationally, she argued inwardly. She did enjoy his company, but that didn't mean there was any deeper meaning to their meeting. Or to the fact that they seemed very compatible in many areas. Given her aversion to city slickers like

Wilbur, however, she saw no reason to shun the amiable, good-looking cowboy. As long as Ryan was in town, she could enjoy his company and perhaps discourage her father's matchmaking, if only for two or three weeks.

She would never lead a man on, of course, which meant she would have to tell Ryan all about her dad and why she was unwilling to heed his wishes. A smile slowly lifted the corners of her mouth. It could actually be fun to pretend the handsome rider was her boyfriend, particularly if he was in on the ruse and knew all about her father's crazy efforts to get all his kids married off and settled on nearby ranches of their own.

Tonight, at the fireworks show, she would set up the amusing scenario. Talk about *fireworks!*

If Ryan shows up, she added silently.

He will. Julie was positive. And since she was going to be back on the ranch soon, she'd freshen up before returning to town for the evening festivities.

Especially the bull riding. She couldn't miss that. She'd promised Ryan she'd be there for as many of his rides as possible, and she intended to keep her word.

A warmth infused her cheeks as the reality of the situation grew clearer. Hers was more than a simple friendly promise. She truly wanted to be present to watch him ride. And to pray for his safety when the chute gate opened and he spent the next eight seconds, and beyond, in mortal danger.

Closing her eyes as her brother drove toward home, Julie began her prayers for Ryan's safety then and there.

He'd come in third in the first round of saddle-bronc riding and had hit the ground right in front of one of the TV cameras, so his landing was liable to wind up on the late news. This ride hadn't earned the best score he'd ever been awarded, but it wasn't the worst either, and there were more chances coming in the ensuing days. They'd eliminate some of the less able riders this first weekend, add some special former champions the second, then tie up the titles and grand prize money during the third and final series of events. All he had to do was see that he landed in the top ten this weekend, then wait for the next chance and the next and do the same.

By the time it was all over, he expected to have lined his pockets with plenty of money and maybe come away with a new hand-tooled saddle and bridle, a pair of silver spurs and a couple of fancy buckles, too.

Barnyard aromas permeated the air. Dust rose in clouds as the livestock was shifted from place to place by expert wranglers. The sun overhead beat down on men and animals alike.

Ryan mopped his brow and donned a protective vest. He'd seen his first bull perform before, so he wasn't going into this ride blind. He squared his hat on his head tightly and scaled the fence to prepare to step aboard.

One last look at the cowboys and groupies gathered behind the chutes was all it took to make him smile and hesitate. Julie was back!

She waved her arm wildly and grinned. "Hi!"

Acknowledging her with a nod, Ryan stood astride the chute fences, holding his weight off the animal while friends pulled his rigging tight for him and he rubbed his rosined gloves along the braided poly-and-manila rope. He slipped his glove through the handhold, laid the braid across his palm and took his wrap. Then he pounded his stiff fingers tighter with his free hand and eased himself down onto the bull's back.

This brindle had a hump like a Brahma cross and horns big enough to reach out and touch a guy if he wasn't careful.

Ryan pulled his feet off the rails. Nodded to signal the gate man. Held his breath. Raised his free hand over his head and tensed, ready for anything—he hoped.

The bull turned toward the arena, leaped into

the air, landed stiff legged and was airborne again before even one second had passed.

There was no way to calculate the time or plan ahead. All Ryan could do was keep his balance, bend at the hips to stay out over the shoulders of the snorting, slobbering, lurching animal and hang on.

The crowd went wild, screeches, hoots and cheers buoying him up.

Focused so intently on the bull, Ryan barely heard anything beyond the animal's growls and the roar of the spectators in the stands.

Julie was perched on the top rung of the arena fence, shouting, "Go, go, go! Yes!"

An air horn sounded. The eight seconds were up. He'd made it!

"Yay!" Her heart was already pounding from the excitement when she saw Ryan reaching for his rope to loosen it.

"Oh, no! His balance is off," she yelled to nobody in particular. He was slipping to one side. And the bull was still bucking just as hard as it had before.

Julie gasped and held her breath. The crowd reacted the same way. The din behind her changed to a more muted reverberation. Tension was palpable.

Bullfighters in clown makeup and baggy clothes

dashed into the fray. One headed straight for the bull, reaching out as if planning to touch its forehead between the curved horns.

Ryan finally pulled his hand free. He leaped, landing in the dirt and rolling aside, barely escaping the pounding cloven hoofs of the immense animal.

Julie screamed. Men were shouting.

Ryan clambered to his feet, raised his arms over his head and bounced on his toes like a prize-fighter after scoring a knockout.

She caught his eye almost immediately and watched his elated grin broaden even more. By the time he'd scooped up his hat and been handed his discarded rigging, he was almost to the fence where she'd been waiting.

"Great ride!"

He beamed. "Thanks."

"Lousy dismount, though. I thought you were a goner for sure."

"Nah, he missed me by a mile."

"Try a few inches. Why don't you at least wear a helmet like so many of the other riders do?"

"Can't see well enough through the face mask," Ryan replied. "Besides, it throws off my balance."

"It's still better than getting your head stomped flat. Do you have any idea how close you came just now?"

"He missed, didn't he?" One eyebrow arched. "Well?"

She gave him an exaggerated pouting look. "Yes. This time he did. What about the next time? Or the time after that?"

"Worried? Careful, or folks will think you care."

"I do."

"What about all that talk of praying for me?"

"I did. I was. But that doesn't mean you can't still get hurt."

"Then why bother?"

Although he seemed nonchalant and carefree about it, Julie sensed an underlying sense of seriousness, as if he wanted an honest answer.

"Sometimes I wonder about that myself," she confessed. "But I keep in mind that the Bible says to pray without ceasing and to ask for anything we want."

"Sounds like a kid writing to Santa."

Sobering, she shook her head. "Not at all. It's a connection with our faith, with God and Jesus, that helps me all the time, no matter what answers I get."

"Really?"

His arched eyebrows and evident skepticism were disturbing but not enough to dissuade her. "Yes, really. As a believer, if I trust God to do what's best for me and try to listen and stay in

His will, then I'll know what to pray for and He'll help me achieve it."

"If you say so."

"I do." Forcing a smile, she looped her hand around his elbow and fell into step beside him. "I know where they stashed the leftovers from the picnic. Are you hungry now that your rides are over for the day?"

"I could eat."

"Good. Stow your gear and we'll go rustle up some food before the fireworks show starts."

Ryan glanced at the sky, then back at her. "It's a while until dark."

Laughing lightly, Julie agreed. "So we'll have lots of time to get to know each other better. And I promise I won't always talk about sheep."

"Well…" His drawl was enchanting and his expression amusing. A lopsided grin turned up one corner of his mouth and his eyes twinkled despite being shaded by his hat brim.

"If you promise."

Julie followed him to a heavy-duty red pickup truck that was parked near the fairgrounds camping area. "Nice. Is this your rig?"

Nodding, Ryan carefully stowed his gear bag inside the matching camper shell next to the saddle and halter he used for bronc riding and checked everything before slamming the door. He paused beside the truck. "I should have brought a change of shirts. I thought I had another clean one in my truck, but I was mistaken."

"You'll do just as you are," Julie told him, brushing off his shoulders as she spoke. "This is just dust." She snickered. "Thankfully."

"Hey, you're a ranch girl. You should understand what sometimes happens when we fool with animals." She saw him eyeing her outfit. "I see you changed. Too much wool?"

"Something like that." She was not about to tell him that she'd put on the plaid, ruffled, Western shirt in order to try to impress him. It was bad enough to have done so in the first place without actually admitting it.

"Well, you look very nice. The blue you had on before really matched your eyes, though."

He'd noticed? Uh-oh. Was that good—or bad? Not that it mattered, Julie reasoned. If she intended to teach her father a lesson and still play fair with this attractive cowboy, she'd better speak her piece soon, before he laid on the charm any more heavily.

As soon as he'd closed and locked the cab of the truck, as well as the camper shell, she took his arm again. "Come on. We'll go over to the storage room behind the snack bar and raid the fridge while I explain a few important things to you."

Ryan pulled back just enough to stop her. "Like what?"

"For a guy who's not worried about facing a rampaging bull, you sure scare easily when it comes to people. Don't worry. I just need a little favor from you. It won't hurt a bit."

"That's what a sports medic told me just before he twisted my dislocated shoulder back into place last year in Cheyenne. Maybe you'd better explain what's up before we go any further."

"I need a boyfriend," Julie said, bursting into laughter at the startled look on Ryan's face. "To teach my father a lesson. And I think you're just the man for the job." She giggled more. "It's only for a couple of weeks."

"You go through boyfriends that fast?"

"Actually, no," she admitted, blushing in spite of herself. "I'm not normally very social. I'm too busy working and tending to my flock. I'm the baby of the family, so I don't understand why Dad is in such a big hurry to marry me off, but he is. I just thought it would be funny, plus give me a break from the pressure he and my mother have been putting on me, if he believed I was interested in somebody like you."

"Me? Why me?"

"Well, I do like you. And we have run into each other several times since you came to Jasper Gulch. What will it hurt?" She released him abruptly and stepped back. "Unless you have somebody special already. Do you? That barrel racer, maybe?"

"I told you. Bobbi Jo and I are just friends."

"Then you'll do it? You'll pretend we're dating?"

Ryan shook his head and arched his eyebrows. "You really cut to the chase, Miss Shaw. Let's say I agree to hang out with you between events. How do I know my actions won't cause your dad to throw me out of the rodeo?"

"He wouldn't do that. He might yell at me a lot, but you'll never know he's upset. Appearances are very important to him. So is his sterling reputation. Mayor Jackson Shaw would *never* let his emotions get the better of him, especially not in public. Look how calm he stayed when they opened the vault and the time capsule was gone."

"That's true. He did handle himself—and the crowd—very diplomatically. It was the TV reporters who got excited."

"That's their job," Julie said. She offered her hand. "Then it's a deal?"

"Deal," Ryan replied.

He grasped her hand tenderly and with more finesse than she had anticipated. His skin was warm yet callused, and restrained strength seemed to flow from his fingertips like currents of electricity.

For the first time since she'd hatched her plan to thwart her father, she was asking herself if she'd made a terrible mistake. They were merely shaking hands to seal a bargain, yet there was something different about this contact. Something special. Something so extraordinary it was indescribable.

If she'd been able to step back in time and return to that morning, she wondered if she'd have had enough sense to stand her ground instead of changing vantage points at the parade and encouraging him to notice her.

Would she do anything different if she had another chance? The question stuck in her mind until her cheeks were rosy again.

Standing there beside him in the midst of the fairgrounds parking lot, with people milling around and plenty of background noise, she felt as if she and Ryan were alone in the wilderness. While he held her hand, there was no one else who mattered. And no way to make herself step away to break the intimate mood, either.

Worse, she imagined the same reactions, the same feelings, emanating from him. Was it possible that he was as stupefied about their emotional connection as she was?

Of course not. Julie huffed, grinned, pulled away and changed the subject. "Okay. Time to eat. I'm starved."

She'd have felt a lot more at ease if she hadn't

immediately recalled the old saying, "The way to a man's heart is through his stomach."

Well, at least I'm not taking advantage of him, she reasoned. They liked each other, so why not make the most of the next few weeks and get to be friends? What could that hurt? Besides, keeping steady company with Ryan meant she'd be too tied up for her parents' efforts at matchmaking.

That alone was worth a little innocent misdirection.

Chapter Six

Ryan drove Julie to the Beaver Creek Bridge and parked as close as Rusty Zidek's hunter-orange–vested crew would permit. Circling the truck, he helped her down and followed as she made her way toward the rusted iron span.

"This is the old bridge your town plans to refurbish?"

She nodded. "Some of us hope to. My brother Cord is on the town council committee to raise money for repairs so we can eventually reopen it to vehicle traffic."

"You sound as if you're not sure that will happen."

"It would help if my dad wasn't so determined to slow down progress. Considering all the other things he's done for the benefit of Jasper Gulch, it's hard to understand what his problem is with fixing up the bridge."

"Maybe it's about the cost."

"That's part of it, of course. Lots of people think the legend of Lucy Shaw should be played up more, too. You know, for tourist appeal."

"That's a new one on me," Ryan said. "Who's Lucy Shaw, a relative of yours?"

"My great-great-aunt. She was killed when she drove off this very bridge in her daddy's Model T, landed in the creek and drowned."

"That's pretty sad, if you ask me. Why do you think it's so interesting?"

"A couple of reasons. One, it happened in 1926, so it's ancient history. And two, Lucy's body was never recovered. Since she was the daughter of the town founder, Ezra Shaw, everybody and his brother turned out to search for her."

"Surely they would have found her, then."

"Not necessarily. It had been raining heavily for days and the creek was flooding over its banks. There were rapids for miles instead of the ripples that we can see from here. Plus, this country was a lot wilder at that time. Predators could have destroyed any sign of her before rescuers had time to travel far enough."

"I suppose that's plausible."

"It's the accepted theory. Anyway, old Ezra was never the same after losing his daughter. He shunned the bridge, so almost everybody else did, too. It's been painted occasionally and has had some other basic maintenance done, but nowhere near the depth of work that needs to be finished before we can legally open it to normal traffic. My brother Cord has all the specs and knows what to do, but getting a firm promise of funding has been impossible."

"So he's using this centennial celebration as an added motivation?"

Julie nodded. "Yes. We're hoping that when the holdouts like Dad see the benefits of tourism, they'll change their minds and not try to keep the modern world at bay. That's what Ezra ended up doing, even if he didn't look at it that way."

"Oh, I don't know. He bought a Model T."

"Exactly. And he blamed the car for Lucy's death, too. From then on he refused to have anything to do with new inventions. He drove a horse and buggy for the rest of his life. Wouldn't set foot in another motor vehicle."

"That's incredible." Ryan was delighted to see her smile again.

"I know. There are always folks who hate progress. Take my wool customers, for example. They wouldn't have to spin their own yarn, but I'm in business because enough serious hobbyists insist on doing it by hand."

"There's a difference," Ryan said. "They do it because they choose to, not because they have scarred memories like Ezra did."

As soon as that statement was out of his mouth, Ryan realized how well it could apply to him, to his basic reasons for living a life on the road.

I'm different, he argued, wishing he could get through just one day without feeling pangs of guilt over his only brother's death. *I was just a kid. Kirk was older and should have known better.*

And I should have told Mom what he'd been doing, Ryan countered silently. *If I had, he might still be alive.*

A gentle tap on his arm brought his thoughts back to the present. Julie was studying him intently.

"What's wrong?" she asked. "I hope my story about Lucy didn't depress you?"

"Not at all." He shook off his private memories and took her hand. "C'mon. We need to go stake out a good spot on the bridge to watch the fireworks. And to be seen by your family while we snuggle."

Even in the lower light from the setting sun he could see that her cheeks had reddened again. A young woman who blushed was a rarity in his experience and he found that trait endearing.

"You don't have to overdo it," she whispered. "I didn't mean…"

He chuckled. "I know. I was just kidding. If you get chilly, you can always borrow one of the jackets I keep in the truck for emergencies."

When she answered with a disheartened-sounding "Oh," Ryan laughed even more heartily. Since he clearly didn't understand women, this one in particular, he figured he may as well just roll with the changes in her mood the way he let a bucking horse or bull influence his countermoves. That way, when their time together was up and he moved on, he'd still be in one piece.

The last thing he wanted to do, would allow himself to do, was let down his guard and leave a piece of his heart behind in Jasper Gulch.

Julie led the way onto the bridge and chose a spot far from the section where her family always gathered. The actual span wasn't that long, perhaps the length of a football field or two. There was plenty of room for spectators as long as they didn't mind being a little crowded.

A surprising shiver tickled her spine and made her fingers and toes tingle. She sensed Ryan's nearness, felt his arm come to rest across her shoulders as he asked, "Are you cold?"

"No. I'm fine." Although it was her intention to lean away from him, she found herself held tight. "Really. I'm not a bit chilly."

"I know," he drawled. "But we seem to be the object of interest to so many people, I hate to disappoint them."

"My family? Can you see them?"

"If your dad wears a black felt hat and your mom and sister like straw the way you do, then yes, I think I do. What convinced me is the stir we caused over there when I started to try to keep you warm."

"I'm plenty warm right now, thank you," she said with a nervous giggle. "I'm sure it's still in the high seventies."

"Meaning, I should stop hugging you?"

"That's probably for the best," Julie admitted wryly. "I don't want Mom picking out long white dresses and bridal bouquets just yet."

"Now, *that's* a scary thought," Ryan whispered in her ear before releasing his hold and easing away.

"I know. I'll be glad when some of my siblings give up and find mates so our parents can relax."

"I saw your dad and mom on the stage at the bandstand. Were the others all related to you, too?"

"No. Some were dignitaries Dad invited. I have three brothers. Cord is thirty-four, Austin is thirty-two and you met Adam when he was helping me with my sheep. He's the youngest brother. Twenty-nine."

"That's right. He called you Little Bo—"

Her elbow nudged him in the ribs. "You'll forget you heard that nickname if you know what's good for you."

"Yes, ma'am. What about your sister? Is she older than you are?"

"Yes. Faith is twenty-seven."

"Please tell me you're over eighteen," Ryan begged, acting a bit uneasy.

Julie had to laugh. "I'm twenty-four."

"You don't look it."

"I guess you mean that as a compliment, so I'll take it that way. Faith keeps telling me I need makeup to cover my freckles, and fancier clothes, but I'm comfortable in Western wear. Besides, it's a lot more practical on the ranch."

"Hey, I like cowgirls."

"Especially barrel racers?"

"Nah. They're too fast for me."

It took Julie a couple of heartbeats to realize he was teasing her again. She grinned up at him. "Clever."

"*I* thought so."

She couldn't help but appreciate his exaggerated self-confidence. His dark eyes twinkled in the fading light and the tiny scar in the cleft of his chin gave him a roguish appearance.

When she said, "I have no doubt you did," her reward was the sound of the cowboy's sincere laughter.

It had been years since Ryan had lingered anywhere to watch fireworks. Pyrotechnics were often used to excite the crowds at rodeos, especially as a preliminary to special bull-riding events, but that was nothing compared to the show this little town was putting on.

There were static displays along the creek banks that alternated with aerial explosions, sending glittering, burning, colored bits in all directions. Some actually rained down from the sky like showers of falling stars.

"Oh, wow!" Julie exclaimed again and again between contented sighs and bouts of applause. "So beautiful."

"Certainly is." He knew she meant the fireworks. And he could have kept his personal opinions to himself. Probably should have, he decided, when she whirled and stared up at him. Although he had not made any specific reference to her, she seemed to sense his double meaning.

Smiling, he tilted the brim of her hat back with one finger to better gaze into her eyes. There was no retracting his statement now. Not considering the way she was already responding. "It's fun watching you enjoy yourself so much. I'd forgotten how great small towns can be at times like these."

"Right. Okay, then. As long as you're not forgetting our deal."

Ryan bent to speak softly, privately, removing his hat to facilitate the closeness. "I remember you wanted me to convince your father that I was your boyfriend. Am I not living up to our bargain?"

Instead of replying, Julie pivoted back to concentrate on the fireworks display as the finale launched with a crescendo. Shell after shell exploded over the creek. The air was electric with excitement, filled with the odor of gunpowder propellant that left clouds of smoke in its wake.

Ryan felt a shiver of unexplained elation himself, quickly dismissing it as nothing more than shared enthusiasm radiating from the crowd.

And from Julie, he reminded himself. Especially from her. That was the problem. In the past few hours he had felt more and more of his protective shell cracking, more of his total control slipping away, as if being with Julie was opening his eyes to possibilities he had never before considered.

That was patently ridiculous, of course. He knew exactly who he was and what he was doing with his life. He was happy. Well, contented at least. He hadn't missed out on anything by riding in rodeos. On the contrary, there were thousands of erstwhile cowboys who would give anything to be in his boots. He was competing all over the country, standing near the top of the point charts and winning regularly enough to live comfortably, send money home to help his single mother, Carla, and still build up a decent savings account.

So what's my problem? Ryan asked himself.

He didn't like the answer he got because it came in the form of an urge to put his arms all the way around Julie, lean forward and start to whisper in her ear once more, then go ahead and kiss her.

You want to. You know you do, his conscience insisted.

And that's the perfect way to make her tell me to get lost, he countered. He could use that as an excuse if he truly did want to stay away from her. Or, he could back off, behave himself and spend a lot more time with her.

He wished he could have credited himself with totally noble motives, but he could not. Yes, he would continue to behave like a gentleman because he was one. But that didn't mean he was doing it for the right reasons. Truth to tell, he yearned to spend time with this special young woman and would have done almost anything to keep from upsetting her.

Relaxing because he'd come to a sensible decision, Ryan continued to watch the fireworks show. Later, if he deemed it necessary, he'd probe the reasons for his actions and try to figure them out.

For now, he was simply going to be himself—an itinerant rodeo rider who was there one day and gone the next. That way there would be no surprises. The only things he'd have to worry about were the bucking horses and bulls he was going to face in the coming weeks. That was the only part of his future that really mattered.

As the smoke drifted away and the crowd began to move, Julie lightly touched his sleeve. "Are you okay?"

Displaying his trademark grin, Ryan squared his hat on his head and nodded. "I'm fine."

"Okay, you just seemed a little down."

"Not me," he vowed, taking her hand as they strolled off the bridge. "I've never felt better."

The instant he spoke, he knew it wasn't true. Part of him did feel wonderful, but there was also an inner turmoil he could not explain. Nor was he ready to probe any deeper into his thoughts. Some regrets were best left buried with the memories of the people who had caused them.

Julie had no desire to leave Ryan that evening. If she had not had chores to do at home and animals who counted on her, she would have lingered in town.

"Where can I drop you?" Ryan asked.

"I brought my truck back to town after Adam and I took my sheep home. It's parked at the rodeo grounds."

"Okay. How about a cup of coffee first?"

"Not if I hope to get to sleep tonight," she replied.

"Decaf?"

Julie chuckled softly. "That seems rather point-less, doesn't it? I drink the stuff for the caffeine."

"Yeah, me, too."

"Where are you staying while you're compet-ing?" She hoped he wasn't going to tell her he was camped next to the barrel racer—not that she was a bit jealous.

"There were no rooms here in town. I thought I was going to have to bunk in my truck until that friend of yours—Hannah?—pointed me to a dude ranch that was renting out their bunkhouses."

"Several ranches took in riders and livestock. We didn't have enough pens at the fairgrounds to bed down all the animals. That's another reason why I hauled my sheep home. It's not really far to the ranch from here."

"I'd like to see your operation sometime, if you feel like showing me."

"You would? Dad has cattle, of course. And so do my brothers. But all I have is sheep."

"That's okay. I'll cope."

"I'm surprised you haven't been teased about me and my sheep already."

Ryan laughed. "Who says I haven't?"

"I'm so sorry."

"Don't worry. I can take it. I have broad shoul-ders."

She said, "I noticed" before she could stop her-self. Instead of getting serious, he only laughed more, particularly when she buried her face in her hands.

"Glad to hear it," he quipped. "I'd hate to have your family and friends feeling sorry for you because you're hanging out with an ugly cowhand."

"I think I'm safe there," she said, thankful that he was in such an upbeat mood again. "You're a big step up from the men my dad has been trying to get me interested in. I feel sorry for some of them, but not sorry enough to break down and date them. Besides, it wouldn't be fair to encourage a guy I'd never marry."

"I suppose you could look at it that way," he drawled. "How about just having a little fun, like we did tonight? That's innocent enough, isn't it?"

"I guess so."

Julie bit her lip. She truly had intended her time with Ryan Travers to be casual. The trouble was, her imagination had quickly moved from mere interest in friendship to thoughts of wanting more. Of wanting him to like her and Jasper Gulch enough to decide to hang around.

Yes, she was kidding herself. And yet, if the good Lord had brought them together, even for a short time, perhaps He had something in mind.

At this point, all Julie could do was take a deep breath, bide her time and continue to pray for Ryan as she'd promised. *That* she could do without feeling awkward. However, if her prayers began to drift into the area of their personal relationship, she was going to have to counteract them somehow.

That notion amused her. Here she was, supposedly trusting God with her current life as well as her future. Therefore, her prayers should be that His will be done and that she be aware of it so she didn't make a mistake.

I think I already did, she admitted to herself. *I like this cowboy way too much for my own good.*

All she had to do was keep her cool if she wanted to find out where their pretend relationship might be headed. Considering that she already had a crush on the handsome rider, that was *not* going to be as easy as it sounded. Not even close.

Chapter Seven

By Sunday afternoon, many of the first week's competitors had been eliminated. Ryan's cumulative scores were among the top ten in all three of his events, so he'd qualified for the semifinals.

He should have been happy. And he was, with one exception. The whole morning had passed without his seeing Julie. By this time he was thinking of her far too much and missing her every moment they were apart, which really shook him up. How she had managed to get under his skin so completely in such a short time was not only amazing, it was clear scary.

When he spotted her coming toward him, he felt his heart speed the way it did every time the chute gate opened. "Ridiculous," he muttered, grinning at her in spite of himself.

Julie waved and picked up her pace, so she was beside him quickly. "Hi. How's it going?"

"Fine. I wondered what had happened to you."

The puzzled look she gave him was short-lived. "Oh, I get it. Because I wasn't here earlier?"

Ryan nodded.

"I always go to church. I'm sorry I didn't mention it in time for you to go with me. I should have." She brightened. "But there's always next Sunday. And Wednesday nights, for prayer meetings and Bible study."

"That's okay. No harm done."

"Except that I feel bad," Julie told him. "I should have invited you even though you—"

He didn't have to hear it spelled out, so he interrupted. "I know. I didn't sound enthused before. That's okay. I'm not much of a churchgoer anyway."

"It wouldn't hurt for you to give it a try. We have a new, younger pastor, Ethan Johnson. He's the one giving the invocations before each performance of the rodeo. I think you'd like listening to him preach. He's real down to earth." She gently touched Ryan's forearm through his sleeve. "Will you at least think about it?"

"Because your folks will have a conniption to see us together again?"

Julie shook her head and bestowed a smile on him that made him feel weak as a kitten for a moment.

"No," she said softly, tenderly. "Because I'd like you to be there with me."

"Really? Why?"

She was slowly shaking her head. "I don't know. It just seems like it's right, you know? As if I'd be showing you something that's important to me and sharing that part of my life."

"You're going to be showing me the ranch and your sheep. Isn't that enough?"

"No," she said flatly. "It isn't."

The afternoon festivities kicked off with the ropers and steer wrestlers competing first. By the time it was Ryan's turn, Julie was a nervous wreck. She knew better than to anticipate disaster. It was unspiritual. It was also quite human, and she was prone to every one of those failings in spite of her Christian beliefs.

Faith and Hannah had joined her for this part of the competition. They were each holding one of Hannah's young twins, and both Corey and Chrissy had been eating cotton candy.

Julie felt a chubby hand touch and cling to hers. "*Ewww.* Sticky." She held up her nearly empty water bottle. "Here. Let's wash them off before we're all as big a mess as they are."

Faith giggled. "For a girl who has wool fibers floating all over her house and a dog who sleeps at the foot of her bed, you sure are picky."

"Wool brushes off. So does dog hair. Cotton candy melts, as we can all see."

"Speaking of dog hair, how come you didn't bring Cowboy Dan along? I haven't seen him with you since the rodeo started. Aren't you afraid he'll be jealous?"

"He's working. Watching the sheep."

"I thought that's what your Great Pyrenees dogs are for."

"They are. Dan is a born herder and working dog. He'd get bored hanging around here every day, that's all."

"You can't fool me, baby sister. You didn't bring your Australian shepherd pal because you didn't want him to interfere with your budding human friendship."

"Don't be silly."

Hannah was wiping her little boy's hands with a damp napkin before turning to his twin sister. She huffed quietly. "Well, at least you don't have a couple of kids to get in the way of new relationships." Coloring, she added, "Don't get me wrong. I love my kids like crazy and wouldn't change a thing about them, except maybe their time of arrival. Sometimes it seems as if I was pushed so hard to settle down I missed a whole chapter of my life. David and I had almost no time as husband and wife before he shipped out. It's hard to believe he's never coming home."

"How are you doing?" Julie asked tenderly. "I'd

think the kids would help keep you from being too lonely."

"They do. And I'm certainly not ready to consider marrying again. It's just that sometimes, even with Mom and Dad pitching in, my life feels overwhelming." She sighed and straightened after washing the last little hand.

The arena announcer took that moment to begin reading the lineup for the bareback riding. Julie's pulse jumped. Almost Ryan's turn. Another ride. Another risk of life and limb. It was funny how she'd felt so differently about rodeo before she'd had a special someone competing.

Granted, the bull riding was the most dangerous, but those horses were nothing to sneeze at, either. They were big and strong and loved to buck. Some of them were smart, too, meaning they could tell when a rider was off-balance and would adjust their actions to take advantage of his shortcomings and toss him into the dirt.

Once that happened, it was the cowboy's job to make for the fences—if he was able. There were no men on foot to intervene the way they did when bulls bucked. If a pickup man didn't ride to the rescue, it was the competitor's job to save himself.

Trying to appear unconcerned when she wanted to scream for Ryan to be careful, Julie clasped her hands in her lap and sat very still on the hard wooden bleachers. Watching. Waiting. Holding her breath when she saw him climb to the top of the fence at the back of the chutes and push his hat down harder.

"Is that him?" Faith asked.

Julie nodded, her eyes for only one man. "Yes."

"Have you talked to him today?"

"I stopped by after church."

"And?"

Shushing Faith with a wave of her hand, Julie leaned forward, tensing as if she was the one about to leave the chute on the bad-tempered horse. This was a big dun-colored mare with a reputation for trying to stomp her riders flat if she got them on the ground.

Ryan raised his free hand.

Julie was on the edge of her seat, literally.

The gate opened. The clock started.

The audience began to cheer, Julie among them. Others stood and blocked her view, so she jumped to her feet. "Go, go, go!"

A horn blasted to announce completion of eight seconds. Julie was jumping up and down. "Yes! Yes! Hooray!"

At her side, Faith turned to Hannah. "You'd think she liked that guy or something."

The young mother agreed, chuckling and bouncing her children on her knees. "Yeah. You'd think so."

Since they were right, Julie ignored them as

best she could. Was it that obvious? Of course it was. And if her sister and best friend were aware of her feelings, there was a good chance Ryan could tell, too.

Is that a bad thing? she wondered. *Maybe. Maybe not.* A lot depended on whether or not the cowboy's opinion of her had changed. Clearly, she'd gotten off on the wrong foot with him by suggesting they pretend to be a couple. What did that say about her ethics, not to mention her morals? There she was, preaching to him about faith and prayer yet involving him in a farce.

At least it had been make-believe when she'd first suggested it, Julie concluded. Half of it—her half—had turned out to be all too real. The most important question was, what was she going to do about it? How could she possibly explain herself without making Ryan so uncomfortable that he headed for the hills, so to speak?

More honesty was called for. She knew it as well as she knew her own name. And she didn't like the pictures her mind kept creating as the possible result of too much candor.

Ryan collected his day money and looked around for Julie. He'd seen her in the stands with other women and heard her cheering for him, but he'd lost sight of her after the crowd had cleared.

He supposed, given the fact that he wouldn't

be competing again until next Friday night, she might have simply gone back to her normal routine. Which was what he should do, he told himself.

The trouble was, nothing seemed normal anymore unless Julie was included. The plain fact was he missed her. He'd already stowed his bareback rigging and bronc saddle in his truck. Now he put his leather gloves and bull rope into a smaller gear bag, grabbed his chaps and headed for the area where he and the other riders had parked. There was still plenty of activity back there, including the old guy in the Mule who was scooting around barking orders to other gray-haired men wearing fluorescent vests.

The Mule roared by, then stopped ahead of him. Ryan kept walking and caught up.

"Evenin'. You lookin' for a pretty gal with freckles and red hair?" the old man asked.

"Not just any girl," Ryan replied with a slight smile. "Have you seen Julie?"

"Yup." He jerked a thumb over his left shoulder. "She was headed this way from the grandstands about ten minutes ago. Does she know what your truck looks like?"

Ryan nodded. His smile broadened. "Yes."

"In that case, I reckon she's lookin' fer you, too." The tone of his voice dropped and he ran a hand over his thick mustache before he added,

"You'd best treat that gal right or you'll have more than her brothers after your hide. Get my drift?"

"Yes, sir." Amused but also touched that the old man would stick up for Julie, Ryan tipped his hat. "Message received and noted."

"Just so we understand each other."

It occurred to Ryan to mention that Julie and he had been pretending to be a couple. Then he realized that that was no longer so, at least not for him. Thankfully, she was aware that any relationship they might develop would be short-lived. It had to be. He was going to stick around for a couple more weeks, providing he kept winning and qualified for the finals, but after that he'd hit the road again.

Therefore, he reasoned, it was best that Julie kept assuming he was *not* getting serious about her. He would have given all of his hand-tooled, gold-and-silver prize buckles to have that actually be true.

Locating Ryan's red pickup truck wasn't hard. Julie knew where he usually parked, and since the lot was well lit it was easy to find, even at dusk.

She cupped her hands around her eyes to peer into the camper shell. His special bucking saddle and some other gear was in there, but she suspected he hadn't had time to stow the bull rope and chaps yet.

"What I should have done was wait at the back of the chutes and catch him there," she muttered, knowing full well why she had not done so. She was beginning to get cold feet, not to mention a roaring guilty conscience.

That's what happens when a person stops being totally honest, she decided. It made no difference that her motives were innocent. She had told a fib. Worse, she had involved Ryan in her plot. Both were wrong, but she had an idea that drawing him into it was worse than simply making her own mistakes.

"Hey! What're you doing to my truck?" boomed at her out of the twilight.

Julie jumped back. "I wasn't—"

He was already laughing at her. "Simmer down. Rusty thought I'd find you out here. Why didn't you come by to congratulate me after my last ride?"

"I didn't want to embarrass you in front of your friends." Despite her attempts to quell her errant emotions, she could feel her cheeks beginning to burn.

"Embarrass me?" Ryan continued to chuckle as he opened the back of the camper shell and tossed in the last of his gear. "Honey, they might have been envious, but believe me, I would never be embarrassed to be seen with you." Pausing, he slammed the door and turned to face her. "Are you sure it's not the other way around?"

"Of course not."

"I don't know. That father of yours can be pretty formidable. Some of the riders were talking about the way he's taken charge of this town and is so determined to run it his way."

"That has nothing to do with me," Julie insisted. She could not tear her gaze from his if she wanted to. Even without bright light for reflections, Ryan's eyes glittered like black diamonds. His aura was one of sheer power, yet tempered with underlying gentleness and grace that took her breath away. She began to feel as if she'd been aboard a bucking bull with him and was so spent, so unsteady, she needed to lean on him for support or fall at his feet.

Ryan lightly cupped her shoulders with both hands. "Fair enough. I suppose he would tend to be wired, particularly over the loss of the time capsule. Has there been any word on it?"

"No. Nothing. It's strange that nobody's come forward with information. You'd think someone in a town as full of busybodies as this one would have seen something suspicious. I mean, the site is behind the bandstand in that grove of trees, so it's not as if the capsule was buried out in the middle of nowhere."

"The sheriff's office has no leads?"

"They say not." She shrugged, taking care to not disturb his hands. "I imagine, even if they did, they'd keep it to themselves until they'd had time to properly follow up on clues. Dad sort of suspects Ellis Cooper, the guy he beat out for the mayor's job, but there's no proof."

"I see." Stepping back, he bestowed a quizzical, lopsided smile. "So, Ms. Shaw, are you going to turn me down again if I offer to buy you a cup of coffee?"

"Nope. I'd love a cup. As a matter of fact, some of us were planning to meet at the café in town. We'd love to have you join us."

"That's not exactly what I had in mind, but it'll do. Will your father be there, too?"

"No. He and Mom headed home right after Sunday-evening services."

"Church? Again? You didn't go?"

She had to give in and smile or burst. "Not this time. I tried to talk the pastor into delaying until after the last bull ride, but he didn't think much of that idea."

"You *didn't!*"

Julie was shaking her head and giggling. "Of course not. I may be a dyed-in-the-wool rodeo fan but I have my limits."

"Is that another sheep joke?"

"I guess you could look at it that way. It is

amazing how many common sayings are related to sheep ranching."

Opening the passenger door of his truck and standing back, Ryan said, "It seems wrong to use the words *sheep* and *ranching* together. A ranch should mean cattle."

"Spoken like a man from Ezra's time," Julie countered. "There's room in Montana for both."

"Only if you happen to have a father who owns the biggest spread in these parts and is willing to let you graze part of it down. How much supplementation do you have to do for top production?"

"The ewes get extra rations before lambing and I keep it up until their babies are weaned."

"I really am looking forward to touring your operation. It'll be four days before I have to ride again. Would it be okay if I spent a day or two just following you around?"

"As long as you work, not just stand there."

"Okay, but no secret filming. I don't want my buddies to see me sheep wrangling on some viral internet video."

"Would I do that?" she crooned.

Ryan laughed. "My personal opinion? In a heartbeat."

Chapter Eight

Great Gulch Grub, across Shaw Boulevard from the bank, was crowded when Ryan and Julie arrived. She'd had him drop her at her truck so she could drive herself into town rather than return to the fairgrounds later for her pickup.

"Besides, the café is on the way home for me," Julie had told him convincingly. He had to accept her choices or find himself classed as a manipulator like her father. Why an otherwise intelligent man didn't see how his actions were alienating his children was puzzling. Even if the mayor did basically run the town, that was no reason for him to try to control the lives of his grown children.

Of course, Ryan concluded as he hurried to join Julie at the door to the quaint restaurant, Shaw had done a pretty good job so far. His kids seemed like level, good citizens, a credit to his parenting skills, which was more than Ryan could say for his own upbringing.

He reached past Julie to open the heavy glass door for her before she could do it herself. Although she looked a bit surprised, she permitted his gallantry.

"I get the feeling you're the independent type," he joked. "I hope I haven't offended you."

"I'm not so progressive I'm silly about it," she replied. "It's just that I'm used to doing things for myself, not that I'm too stubborn to let somebody be nice to me."

"That's good to know." Before he could follow her, a blond teenage girl flounced past and into the café.

Ryan's brows arched as he rejoined Julie. "Who was *that?*"

"Lilibeth Shoemaker. She was a runner-up for Miss Jasper Gulch. She's been in a snit ever since she found out Alanna Freeson beat her."

Julie paused to scan the room. "Oh, what a shame. The tables are all taken. I guess you and I will have to find a separate place at the counter."

"Works for me. If your family wants us to join them in that booth, they'll have to send somebody home to make room, right?"

"My thoughts exactly."

As Julie weaved her way between tables, Ryan took in the scene. The café was clean but obviously old. Wagon wheels holding hurricane lamps hung from the tin-clad ceiling, as did a few fans. The floor was comprised of squares of beige tile and it looked as if many of the tables had been cleaned so often that portions of their embedded finish had been worn away.

The stool Julie chose left only her right side open, so Ryan quickly laid claim to the spot. Looking past her, he realized who their fellow diner was.

Ryan tipped his head politely and Rusty Zidek did the same.

"I see you two found each other again," Rusty drawled. "Can't say I'm surprised."

"It was a good rodeo tonight, wasn't it?" Julie offered.

"That it was." He stroked his ample gray mustache as he leaned to peer at Ryan. "I hear you did pretty fair, son."

"Earned a good check. Glad to get it."

"You movin' on, then?"

Ryan shook his head and smiled across at the clever old man. "Nope. I'm entered for all three weekends, assuming I don't get disqualified before the finals."

"Good Lord willing and the creek don't rise," Rusty muttered, turning his attention to the jeans-wearing waitress who happened to be passing with a full coffeepot. "Hey, Mert! Quit jawin' about that missin' time capsule and tend to your business. My cup's clean empty."

The middle-aged woman tossed her dark curls and shot Rusty a glance that was part affection, part cynicism. "Hush, you old coot. I'll get around to ya." She smiled at Julie. "So has your daddy got any clues?"

"Sorry. No."

"Too bad. It's a mystery all right. Sure has folks riled up." She included Julie's companion in the conversation. "What can I get you two? Coffee? Pie? We got cherry and apple and coconut cream left."

"Just coffee for now," Julie answered. "Myrtle, this is Ryan Travers. He's going to be in town while the rodeo's here, so treat him nicer than you do Rusty, okay?"

Both women laughed, lifting Ryan's spirits even more.

"Will do. Pleased to meet ya," Mert said. "You look like an apple-pie man to me. I'll bring you a slice. On the house."

Dumbfounded to have been accepted so readily and so thoroughly, he nodded. "Thanks. Appreciate it. How about something for Miss Julie, too? I'd hate to eat alone."

"She likes cherry," the waitress told him.

"Then cherry it is. And put ice cream on it if

that's how she usually takes her pie," he replied. "My treat."

The waitress had filled their coffee cups as she'd taken their order. Now she topped off Rusty's mug and elbowed him. "Looks like our Julie's gone and lassoed herself a big spender. You'd better watch out, old man, or he'll steal your girlfriend right out from under your nose."

Rusty gave a hoarse chuckle. "You're my best girl and you know it, Mert. Always have been."

"You're full of it but I love you, too," she said, sashaying over to the glass pie cupboard and stopping to add ice cream to the wedges she was bringing back.

"Friendly bunch of folks," Ryan said aside to Julie. "I can see why you come here to eat."

"That, and it's the only sit-down place in town," she answered. "We can get coffee and fast food at a couple of gas stations but this is more homey."

"Your whole town seems to have the same atmosphere," he said. "It's nice for a change."

"I'm sure you've been in plenty of places like Jasper Gulch."

"Yes and no," Ryan said soberly. He paused to add cream to his coffee and thank the waitress for his pie before he explained further. "I think I feel more at home here because of you."

"Me?"

Ryan nodded. "Yes. You're involved in everything and you know most people by name. That seems strange to me. I usually blow into town, do my job, then pack up my truck and hit the road to the next rodeo. This is the first time in longer than I can remember that I've stuck around enough to really get to know any locals."

"And?"

He shrugged, purposely wanting to appear non-chalant rather than admit how much he was beginning to enjoy the whole experience. "And nothing. I was just making an observation," he said, taking a forkful of pie so he couldn't easily continue their conversation.

A sidelong glance past Julie led him to notice the inquiring look the old man was giving him. Rusty Zidek might be in his nineties, but he was as observant as a man half his age. Maybe more so.

And, unless Ryan missed his guess, that sly old fox could see right through him. That was definitely not good. Not good at all.

Julie could hardly unwind to sleep that night. She was up by dawn and already seeing to her lambs and the ewes with triplets that were still isolated from the main flock. It was more work to handle them separately, but it gave the mamas a better chance of raising all three babies when they received special treatment.

What she'd planned to do was finish her chores,

then go back to her cottage and freshen up before Ryan arrived. That was why, when she'd given him directions to the ranch, she'd told him to come around 9:00 a.m. He caught her in old jeans and a faded blue Future Farmers T-shirt when he drove up a full hour early.

The dogs announced his arrival and circled the truck as if it were a stray member of the flock. Julie's first instinct was to hide in the barn. Quickly realizing that wouldn't help at all, she squared her shoulders and stepped out to meet him.

Grinning and balancing disposable containers, he climbed out of his truck while two immense white dogs and a smaller, mottled gray, white and brown Australian shepherd checked out his tires and sniffed his boots.

"Morning! I brought breakfast. Mert says you like biscuits and gravy." He reached back into the cab for a paper sack. "I brought doughnuts, too, just in case."

"Just in case of what?" Julie was laughing. "Were you expecting to have to feed my whole family?"

"Nope. Only Little Bo Peep."

Julie rolled her eyes dramatically. "I could just strangle Adam for telling you what he calls me."

"Oh, I don't know. I think it's kind of cute." He looked her up and down. "Although right now you look more like Bo Peep's country cousin. I kind of picture her with a dress and a bonnet and that funny curved staff."

"You'll have to wait a long, long time before you catch me in a getup like that," Julie said. She pointed to a charming cottage behind the main house. "I live over there. Let yourself in and put the food on the table in the kitchen. I'll be done with chores in a couple of minutes."

"Can I help you?"

Seeing him standing there in full Western garb, his jeans and shirt clean and pressed, his boots polished, Ryan made Julie feel as if she'd been rolling on the ground by contrast. For all she knew, there were bits of straw caught in her long hair, too.

"No," she said. "You'll get all dirty. I'll finish up. I'm already a filthy mess."

"Am I supposed to argue with you?" Ryan asked with a wry grin.

"Just don't agree out loud," she replied, her face flushing as she dusted off her hands and brushed them over her faded jeans.

"Okay." Turning, he started away.

Julie raised her voice to command, "Cowboy, go to the house," and almost doubled up with laughter when Ryan stopped abruptly and whirled.

"Huh?"

His confused stare explained everything. Trying to stop chuckling long enough to speak, she pointed to the happily spinning Australian shepherd at her feet, then raised her arm toward her cottage. "I was talking to the dog. His name is Cowboy Dan."

"Thank goodness," Ryan responded. "I was afraid I was in trouble already." He grinned broadly and looked to the herding dog. "C'mon, Dan. Let's us cowboys go to the house like Miss Julie wants."

To her shock, the shepherd raced over to Ryan, circled him once and fell into step at his side, as if they'd walked together before and were great pals.

Managing to mute her amused reaction to the dog's obvious adoration of her favorite rodeo cowboy, she muttered, "Oh, no. Not the dog, too."

Ryan's boots made hollow-sounding footsteps on the raised wooden porch of Julie's cottage. Before he could shift his burdens and reach for the doorknob, someone welcomed him. Someone who strongly resembled Julie.

"Hi. Remember me?" Faith stood back and held the door. "Please, come in."

"Dan, too?"

"Of course. He lives here."

"Do you?"

"No. This is all Julie's. I was up at the main house and heard your truck pull in. I knew she wasn't expecting you this early, so I popped over to make sure the place was presentable."

"Looks fine to me. A little woolly, maybe."

"She runs her business from right here," Faith explained, pointing to a stack of clear plastic bags stuffed with raw wool. "It tends to get overly furry from time to time, particularly in the spring when she does most of the shearing."

"Surely not all by herself." Ryan carried the food to the open kitchen and found a place on the table to set it after shoving aside stacks of invoices.

"No, no. She hires it done. She used to do it all back when she had only a few sheep. She'd never keep up these days, not even with electric clippers."

"I'm impressed. She's really a hard worker."

Faith nodded while preparing a fresh pot of coffee. "That she is. As the youngest, I suppose she started out by trying to keep up with the rest of us. Now we all wonder where she gets her energy."

"Where do you work?"

"Here on the family ranch, except when I'm in Bozeman playing in an orchestra. I'm a concert violinist."

"Wow. Aren't you worried about hurting your hands doing ranch work?"

"I'm careful. And I always wear gloves."

"Well, at least you're not a rodeo rider. We tend to get stomped flat from time to time."

"I know. I never have understood why men insist on pitting themselves against animals that are bred for orneriness."

"It's the challenge," Ryan told her.

"It's crazy, but that's only my personal opinion. I have no idea how my sister feels about it. I do know she's on pins and needles every time you ride."

"She is? I knew she was enthusiastic, but I never pictured her as afraid."

Faith faced him and hesitated for a moment before she spoke. "Like I just said, the only time she's scared is for *you*."

If Ryan had been any more surprised, his jaw might have dropped before he could snap it shut. Julie was that concerned? For him? But not as much for other riders?

"Here she comes," Faith said, lowering her voice. "It might be best if you didn't tell her what we've been talking about. I don't want her mad at me."

He totally agreed about keeping their conversation private, only not for the same reasons her sister had cited. Knowing that Julie had become overly concerned for his safety in such a short time was very, very troubling.

Julie burst through the door to her cottage and waved, but she didn't slow down until she'd reached the privacy of her bedroom and bath. Seeing Faith in the kitchen with Ryan had helped. A lot. At least she knew he'd be entertained and wouldn't question her morals since her sister was conveniently present.

She didn't know why she trusted him, but she did. Implicitly. There was something about him that told her it was safe to relax and enjoy his company without surrounding herself with others for reassurance. Nevertheless, she appreciated Faith taking matters into her own hands and visiting at such an appropriate time.

Washed, changed and with her hair brushed, Julie returned to the kitchen. "I hope the gravy stayed hot."

"If it didn't, you can nuke it," Faith said, starting away.

Julie realized her sister was about to leave. "I'm sure there's enough for all three of us," she said, shooting a quick glance at Ryan. "Isn't there?"

"Sure. You said I'd brought enough to feed your family. Faith's more than welcome to share."

"Well, I…"

"Please stay," Julie urged, hoping she didn't sound half as desperate as she suspected she did. "Ryan brought doughnuts, too. I know you love those."

"You just want me to get fat so you'll look thinner," her sister teased. "Three coffees, then?"

"Yes, please." Ryan opened the sacks and spread their impromptu meal on the table while Julie removed another stack of papers to make more room.

"I'm sorry about the mess," she said. "I wasn't expecting to entertain in here or I'd have cleared the table."

"It's fine as long as you don't break out candles and fancy china to try to impress me," he countered. "I'd much rather eat at a kitchen table than have to worry about my manners in an elaborate dining room."

"Your manners are perfect," Julie insisted.

Ryan's grin and twinkling gaze warmed her heart, particularly when he said, "I should hope so. I gave you my best impression of a gentleman."

"Are you telling me you were pretending?" she gibed.

"Let's call it being extracautious," he answered as she slid into a chair between him and her sister. "I didn't want to embarrass you in front of all your town friends."

"Hey, as long as you don't use chewing tobacco like so many cowboys do, you're fine with me."

"Nope. No bad habits."

Across the table Faith chuckled. "That'll be the day."

He arched an eyebrow, purposely overreacting. "I beg your pardon? If you want to share my doughnuts you'd better be nicer to me."

"Yeah," Julie warned with a smile that belied her warning. "Cool it. You're starting to sound like we do when we stand up to our big brothers."

"Do you have brothers and sisters?" Faith asked innocently.

Ryan knew she hadn't meant to probe a tender spot, so he merely shook his head and answered as simply as he could, hoping to stop the questioning without putting a damper on everyone's mood. "I had one brother. Lost him when I was a kid."

"We're so sorry," Julie said.

"No problem." He took a sip from his mug of coffee to buy time until he was certain he had everything under control, particularly his emotions, before he decided to go on and get it over with. "It happened a long time ago. Kirk started drinking in his teens. I should have told Mom, but I thought I owed him my loyalty, so I kept quiet. Eventually, he crashed a car when he was driving drunk and that was that."

"So how did you end up becoming a cowboy?" Julie asked quietly, tenderly.

"Partly because of my brother and partly because of a high school rodeo team. Kirk put me on my first horse. The team trained me later and gave me confidence."

"That's wonderful," Faith said. "I can see where

you might have been so upset, you followed in his footsteps."

Although Ryan didn't comment, he did nod and continue eating so he wouldn't be expected to reply. She was very close to the truth. He had been angry. And lost. And, in his pain, he had struck out at everyone and everything. Alienated drastically, he might easily have ended up on the street, or worse, if a special rodeo coach hadn't taken him under his wing and given him an attainable goal.

The sympathy in Julie's gaze was so touching, so poignant, he refused to acknowledge it rather than show vulnerability.

Instead, he forced a smile, picked up one of the disposable containers and held it out. "More gravy, ladies? There's plenty."

Chapter Nine

"I check my flock at least twice a day, even when they're pastured, and I should go do it soon," Julie told Ryan.

Faith had taken her leave and Julie and he were sitting in the shade on her front porch, having a last cup of coffee while Dan lay at their feet, dozing.

"Okay." Ryan yawned and patted his flat stomach. "Boy, it's a good thing I don't eat that much at breakfast every day or I'd be too fat to ride."

"Hey, you're the one who brought sausage gravy. That stuff is seriously heavy. It sets up like cold oatmeal."

"That's an appetizing image."

He was grinning at her with such an impish glint in his eyes she had to fight harder than usual to keep from blushing. "Did you look at it by the time we'd finished? A spoon would have stood upright."

"Can you cook?" he asked.

The question took Julie by surprise and made her frown. "Why?"

"Just wondered. I didn't see a lot of signs of it in your kitchen."

"I get by. If things get too bad I can always head over to the main house and eat with my family. They have a housekeeper, who also does the cooking. Sandy Wilson. She went to school with Mom."

"Something tells me you don't eat there often."

Julie set her coffee mug aside and stretched. "Nope. I'm too independent, I guess. I'd rather eat crackers and peanut butter at home than dine on filet mignon at my parents' table." Smiling slightly, she eyed him. "Besides, they're always talking politics and it's boring."

"How much political wrangling can there possibly be in a little town like Jasper Gulch? I know your dad's the mayor, but that job should be pretty cut-and-dried."

"It would be if nothing ever changed or wore out or went wrong. Dad does an amazing job balancing the books and getting the most from every tax dollar. I suppose that's why he beat Ellis Cooper in the last election and hung on to his office. Being mayor's a thankless job."

"Any word on the missing time capsule?"

"Not yet. There's plenty of speculation floating around, of course, including a few folks who think Ellis took it just to spite Dad."

"Do you think he did?"

"I strongly doubt it."

"It's hard to believe there's no clue yet. I saw the blowup of the guys getting ready to bury it in the first place. Maybe somebody snapped a picture of the contents before the box went into the ground."

"I'd never thought of that. I'll ask around and see if any of the old-timers have keepsake photos."

"With all the emphasis on history in Jasper Gulch, I can't believe there's no local museum."

"There's been talk of it. Nothing much was ever done to put one together until recently. The town council advertised for an expert, and one of our former locals answered. Olivia—Livvie—Franklin has experience. When she gets here, maybe she'll be able to accomplish more than a few volunteers have so far."

Ryan was nodding sagely. He drained his mug and got to his feet. "Well, I can't help you with history, but I can ride out with you to check your herd."

"Flock," Julie said with a muted chuckle. "Sheep don't come in herds. Remember?"

"Does that mean you can't ride *herd* on them? I've never heard anybody say they rode *flock* on anything."

"You're exasperating, do you know that?"

Doffing his hat and bowing from the waist, Ryan said, "Why, thank you, ma'am. I do my best."

Ryan followed her toward the barn, fully expecting to find a stable of suitable mounts. Instead, she led him to a smaller shed at one side. He balked. "Whoa. Where are the horses?"

"I prefer to just turn a key. By the time I get a horse saddled and bridled and clean its feet, then come back home, curry it and cool it down, the afternoon will be half gone."

"This is *Montana*."

"True, but it's not the early 1900s anymore. And, in spite of Ezra's hang-ups, we have motor vehicles for everything, including riding the range."

"Shameful."

"Practical."

Ryan pulled a face and tilted his hat back with a one-fingered poke at the brim. "What happened to appreciating history?"

"I can recognize the value of the old ways without getting stuck in them, can't I?"

"Well…"

If he hadn't enjoyed teasing her, he would have easily accepted the option of riding ATVs. Since their verbal sparring was so much fun, he decided to continue pretending ignorance.

When she produced two lightweight helmets and handed one to him, he took advantage of the chance to rib her about it. Holding a helmet, he studied it as if it was an alien object. "You don't expect me to wear a sissy hat, do you?"

"It might keep your brains from getting more scrambled than they already are."

He huffed and feigned annoyance. "You think I'm throwing a lasso with no loop?"

"Something like that." Grinning, she tapped the helmet he was holding. "Put it on, cowboy. It won't kill you to take precautions once in a while. I don't know why you don't compete wearing head protection like so many other rodeo cowboys have started doing lately."

"I told you. It throws off my balance."

"Only because you're not used to it. If you practiced…"

"You're a very hardheaded woman, you know that?"

"It has been mentioned in the past, yes."

"By your brothers, no doubt."

To his delight, Julie's smile spread and her blue eyes sparkled. "By just about everybody," she admitted. "My teachers used to write that on my report cards all the time."

"Why am I not surprised?"

She chuckled wryly. "Probably because you already know me better than a lot of folks do. I don't know if you've noticed, but you and I seem to be on the same wavelength most of the time."

"It can seem that way, can't it? I suppose it has to do with our interest in animals and such."

The slow shaking of her head told him more than words when she simply said, "Maybe." Clearly, she knew as well as he did that there was something special going on between them. It wasn't easy to explain or to understand, yet it was undeniably there. An awareness. A camaraderie that had sprung up so quickly it was astounding. And more. Much more.

If he believed in such things, he might actually suspect they were soul mates. He'd encountered and briefly dated other women during his travels. Never had he felt what he felt this time. And never had he sensed this much rapport. This much rightness about a relationship.

That was what this was, Ryan had to admit. He and Julie Shaw already had a personal relationship that had come out of nowhere and had left him reeling. It was impossible. It was foolish.

And it was so real he could almost reach out and touch it.

"My replacement ewes and older females are pastured together. I keep my breeding rams and younger males separate." Julie had pulled her ATV up to a gate and gotten off to open it so the two four-wheel-drive vehicles could pass through. Cowboy Dan was already with the sheep and their enormous white guard dogs, beginning to round them up for her.

Ryan went through the gap first, then dismounted to close the opening behind her.

"Thanks." She left her ATV idling beside his while he latched the gate. "You seem pretty capable for a guy who said he hated riding anything but a horse."

"I may have exaggerated a tiny bit."

"Uh-huh. I thought so. You handle that machine like a pro. The first couple of times I tried to drive this kind of thing I ended up doing wheelies."

The lopsided grin he gave her was telling even before he guessed, "That was no accident, was it?"

Julie had to admit it. "The first one may have been. The second one was to see how far I could go while balanced on the back wheels."

"And you accuse *me* of taking risks!"

"I was twelve. It was before I got smart enough to know better." She eyed the cowboy hat he had refused to remove. "You should have matured, as well."

"I'm all grown up," Ryan argued. "I just have my pride."

"Too much of it, if you ask me," she said over her shoulder as she gunned the engine and accelerated, leaving him in her dust. Since he'd balked at wearing even a simple bike helmet, she knew there was no way she'd ever convince him to forgo his Western hat for the kind of protective gear that was so essential in the rodeo arena. She'd followed the sport for years and was well aware of how many men had either lost their lives or been crippled while competing.

She knew she should not care so deeply, yet she did. In the space of a very short time, Ryan Travers had become the most important person in her life, and it pained her to imagine him hurt. Or worse.

Well, at least he wore a protective vest during all his rides, she reminded herself. That was a start. There had been a time not too many years past when such safety gear did not exist. It had taken the death of a famous, well-liked cowboy to spur one of his fellow competitors to create and perfect a vest that protected the rider's rib cage and internal organs yet allowed him enough flexibility to bend in rhythm with the animal's movement.

Julie's creative mind was spinning wildly when she halted next to the large flock Cowboy Dan was circling and herding toward her.

As soon as Ryan stopped beside her, she said, "I know exactly what guys like you need, and I'm going to invent the perfect piece of rodeo gear just for you."

He arched an eyebrow and peered over at her. "Oh?"

"Uh-huh. I thought of it while we were riding out here. I'm going to call it the Ryan Travers vestie."

"Terrific. I can hardly wait. Enlighten me?"

"It'll be like the vest you already wear, only with an attached hood, like a hoodie sweatshirt. I can line it with fleece padding to protect your head and it can tie under your chin with a pretty ribbon."

The expression on his face was so comical she busted up laughing. "What?"

"You had better be joking."

"Of course. But all kidding aside, you really should consider a real helmet. Even the Brazilian riders are wearing them now."

"Not all of them. A lot of the Aussies haven't changed over, either."

"I take it you're not eager to be on the cutting edge of modern cowboy gear."

"You could say that. I guess I'm kind of like your father about preserving the old ways. After all, they were good enough for our ancestors."

"So were covered wagons and steam engines. I like to think we've outgrown more primitive customs."

Ryan eyed the mottled gray Australian shepherd

that was now running circles around their ATVs. "Did you hear her, Dan? She called me primitive."

"Hey, if the boot fits…"

He couldn't keep a straight face. "You're a very unusual woman, Julie Shaw."

The nod she gave him was emphatic and her expression too funny to overlook.

"I certainly hope so," she declared with a lop-sided smirk and a twinkle in her sky-blue eyes. "I'd hate to think I was wasting all this charm on a guy who wasn't wise enough to appreciate it."

"That does it," Ryan retorted, still pretending to be speaking to Cowboy Dan. "Now she says I'm a wise guy."

Julie was laughing softly when she told him, "You'll get no argument from me about that."

As the day progressed and her visitor lingered, Julie began to wonder what she was going to do about feeding him. The contents of her refrigerator left a lot to be desired, and although she had a couple of steaks in the freezer, it was far too late in the day to try to defrost them properly.

Did rough, tough cowpokes eat peanut butter and jelly sandwiches? she wondered. Or granola bars and yogurt, which made up her usual mid-day meal if she was out of bologna or leftovers? It seemed almost wrong to ask him.

Ryan inclined his head and peered at her from

beneath the brim of his hat. "What's up? You look like you just ate an unripe persimmon."

"That bad, huh?" Sighing, she pulled a face. "It's like this. You brought breakfast and we ate late, but since I'm getting hungry, I figure you must be, too."

He shrugged. "Okay, so?"

"So I wasn't planning on cooking and, believe me, you don't want me to, so how about a peanut-butter-and-jelly sandwich?"

"Why don't you let me treat you to supper in town later instead. The café's open tonight, isn't it?"

"Not usually on Mondays, but I think they extended their hours to accommodate the tourists," Julie said. "I can call and ask. If they're closed tonight, I guess we can grab a pizza at the quick stop on the highway."

"Or eat gourmet PB and Js," Ryan taunted.

"I do have a couple of T-bones in the freezer. Even if I took them out now, they wouldn't be properly defrosted until tomorrow, though. My microwave tends to cook them in the middle when I try to hurry things too much."

The glint in his attractive eyes was almost enough to steal away her breath. When he said, "No problem. We'll eat in town tonight and I'll help you grill those steaks tomorrow night," she felt as if something had siphoned all the usable air out of the entire state of Montana.

He had just invited himself back, and she'd been so dumbfounded she'd let him get away with it. What was wrong with her? She knew she should be upset that Ryan was calling the shots, yet how could she object when he was suggesting exactly what she wanted, too?

The main difficulty was keeping him entertained without appearing too anxious. Yes, she liked having him around. And yes, they did seem to get along well. But that didn't mean he wouldn't get bored following her every day while she tended her flock.

Plus, she needed to check on her knitters, Chauncey Hardman, Carrie Landry, Mamie Fidler and sometimes Sandy Wilson, the Shaw housekeeper. None of them were free to work for her full-time, but Chauncey could always knit when the library wasn't too busy and Carrie had time after she got home from her job as a physician's assistant at the urgent-care center. Mamie's eagerness had been the biggest surprise. Owner and manager of the Fidler Inn, Mamie was so handy with tools and such she'd seemed an unlikely choice to help create scarves, vests and sweaters of homespun yarn. The hourly wages Julie offered were some incentive, of course, but all the women clearly loved to knit.

Warmth crept up her neck and infused her already rosy cheeks when she noticed Ryan waiting for an answer to his suggestion about grilling the steaks. "Well, I suppose…"

"Good. Then it's settled. Do you want me to wait for you here or meet you in town later?"

"Um, meet me later, I guess. I'll need to clean up. I'm pretty dusty."

"Me, too. I'll make a run to the ranch where I'm bunking and grab a quick shower. What time is good for you? Seven?"

"That's fine. If the café is closed when you get there, just park out front and wait for me and we'll go get a pizza together." Not to mention that she'd have to make a serious grocery run, she added to herself. Contemplating a dinner guest the following evening had already made her so nervous her stomach hurt. By the time they actually got around to cooking those steaks, she'd probably have no appetite at all.

"Sounds good," he said easily.

Ryan was standing close enough to reach for her hand, and for a few unsettling moments Julie thought he was going to. Instead, he hooked his thumbs in his pockets and struck a casual pose.

That's exactly what that is, she immediately realized. *It's a pose. He's as nervous about the prospect of being with me as I am about being with him!* What a surprise. And a happy one, at that. If the macho cowboy was having to pretend nonchalance, there was a fair chance he was actually beginning to care what she thought of him. Wahoo! Things were definitely looking up.

Chapter Ten

Ryan was ready and waiting for Julie at Great Gulch Grub by six-thirty.

At a quarter to seven he climbed out of his truck and stood on the sidewalk outside the café. The first few people who passed him to enter the restaurant were so engrossed in their own conversations he might as well have been a life-size chainsaw carving—until Rusty Zidek ambled by.

The old man's smile made his gold tooth glint almost as much as his eyes did. He gave a polite nod, then stopped and joined Ryan where he was leaning against the building's facade. "Evening, son. Lose your lady again?"

"She's supposed to be on her way," Ryan replied. He checked his watch. "It's still early."

"Just keep hummin' that country song about waitin' on a woman."

"Matter of fact, I'd thought of that already." He had to smile and play along. "Want to sing harmony?"

"Not 'specially." Rusty chuckled and fingered his mustache. "Actually, I'm kind of glad to catch you alone. I been wonderin' if your intentions toward Miss Julie are still honorable."

Ryan nearly choked trying to suppress a laugh. The ancient cowboy was clearly dead serious. "I—uh—I have no specific intentions," he stammered. "We just met."

"Yeah, I know. The thing is, I ain't never seed her act so besotted over any man, particularly no cowhand like you."

Displaying a lopsided smile, Ryan said, "Don't let the outfit fool you. I'm not as much a hick as you seem to think I am. I make a real good living riding in rodeos."

"Don't doubt it. If they'd offered that much prize money in my day, I'd have been able to buy me a big spread. Maybe even as big as Shaw's place."

"I never asked Julie how many acres they had," Ryan mused. "It looked pretty impressive, though."

"Oughta be." Rusty coughed aside, then began to chuckle on the same breath. "I've heard it said that Jackson Shaw has more land than God—no offense meant."

"None taken. From what I know about Julie, I

doubt she'd appreciate that comparison, though. She's pretty religious."

Rusty was slowly shaking his head. "Wouldn't exactly put it that way, son. There's a big difference between faith and organized religion, not that I've got anything against church. It's just that puttin' a saddle on a dog don't make him a horse any more than sittin' in church makes a fella a Christian, if you get my drift."

"Not really." Ryan's brow furrowed.

The old man tapped Ryan's chest with a gnarled finger. "It's what's in there, in your heart, that makes the difference. Bein' a Christian is an inside job, not something you can borrow from a friend or inherit from your folks. You gotta get right with God all by yourself."

"I'm afraid I'm not even close," he said, unwilling to tell the old man how disillusioned he was with his Heavenly Father and how much he doubted that God even cared.

Rusty snapped his fingers. "We're all this close to eternity, son. 'Specially a fella like you who risks his life every time he climbs into the chutes. Don't wait too long. When your time's up, it's up."

"Speaking of time, I think that's Julie's truck," Ryan said, glad to have a chance to escape the impromptu lecture on spirituality.

"Sure is. Well, have a nice night," Rusty said. "Will you be stickin' around much longer?"

"Like I said, as long as I keep winning, I'll keep riding. See you next weekend."

"Or before. You remember what I said. We think mighty highly of our Miss Julie in Jasper Gulch. See that you treat her right."

Or else remained unspoken, but Ryan understood completely. He was not the kind of man who led women on or lied to them, so there was no reason for anybody to worry about Julie.

Considering the way he viewed this current situation and the way he was beginning to feel, the only heart in danger of being broken was his own.

Spotting Ryan in front of the café was such a blessing Julie could hardly contain her enthusiasm. He'd not only kept his word, he'd arrived even before she had, and she'd purposely left home early. Perhaps he was starting to be as excited about spending more time with her as she was getting to be near him.

And maybe he'd simply started for town as soon as he was ready, she countered, disgusted to be so over the moon about their date. That's what it was, wasn't it? A date? A real date? This meal was different. At least she assumed as much.

Why? she asked herself.

Because I want it to be. Not a very comforting answer but the truth nonetheless.

Julie parked, then sighed as she climbed out

of her truck. Up until July the Fourth, she would have insisted there wasn't a romantic bone in her body. Now she was so befuddled about her feelings she could barely think straight, let alone behave normally. Keeping a lid on her emotions so she didn't scare Ryan away was crucial. Unfortunately, attempting to do so was giving her an upset stomach and making her hands tremble at the most inopportune times. Too bad he wasn't having the same problem so they could talk about it and make jokes the way they often did about other things.

Cramming her keys into her jeans pocket, she stepped up on the curb and smiled in his direction, noting that he was already coming toward her. The grin on his handsome face was so broad, so appealing, she was certain it was totally genuine. "I hope I haven't kept you waiting."

"Not a problem," Ryan assured her. "Your friend Rusty kept me entertained."

Julie rolled her eyes. "Uh-oh. I hope he didn't tell stories about me. He's known me since I was a baby."

Ryan chuckled, further lifting her spirits. "Nope. I'll have to remember to ask him about your childhood the next time I see him. I imagine he can spin quite a tale."

"You have no idea!" She fell into step beside Ryan and he held the café door for her. The place wasn't as crowded as the last time they'd been there, and she led the way to a corner booth.

As soon as she was seated, Ryan dropped his hat on the empty bench and slid in next to her rather than take a seat across the table. His nearness made her pulse jump and kick like a frisky lamb in a spring meadow. Whatever aftershave he was wearing was just right, not cloying like Wilbur's or too woodsy to suit her. Matter of fact, he was giving off such masculine vibes she was almost dizzy from being so close.

Settling back in the booth, she turned slightly and put her spine into the corner where the booth met the wood-paneled wall. She hadn't meant her movement to be noticeable.

Ryan arched an eyebrow. "Am I crowding you too much? Would you like me to move?"

There was her chance to ask for breathing room. She knew she should take it, yet something stopped her. "I'm fine. Just kicking back. It was a long day."

"You're a hard worker," he said with a nod. "I never dreamed there'd be so much to do keeping a herd—I mean a flock—healthy and happy. I may prefer horses and cattle, but I have to admit, those little guys are cute."

"I know. You should see them when they're newborn. They're more like stuffed toys than barnyard animals."

"I imagine thinking that way can get dangerous at times."

Surprised, Julie agreed. "You're right. The rams, and some of the ewes, can be very territorial. I'm just thankful I'm not in the qiviut business."

"What's that?"

"The undercoat from musk oxen. Alaskan natives gather it when the animals shed. It's supposed to be the world's softest wool, but I think mine is a close second."

"Guess we should all be thankful," Ryan teased. "If the locals aren't crazy about your sheep, they'd probably riot if you brought in a herd of musk ox."

"It's not cold enough here," Julie replied. "Jasper Gulch is safe."

"That's comforting." He signaled to Mert and she hustled back to their booth.

When she recognized her customers, she grinned at the cowboy and winked at Julie. "Good to see you two again. Pie and coffee?"

Julie shook her head. "No. Real food this time." She turned to Ryan. "Their specialty is barbecued ribs. I highly recommend them."

"Sounds good to me. Baked potatoes?"

"And a side salad for me. House dressing. And iced tea," Julie added, not too surprised when Ryan finished his order the same way. Either he was being especially accommodating or they really did have similar likes and dislikes. Did it matter?

Yes. It did matter. A lot. For some unfathomable reason she wanted to learn every way in which hers and Ryan's tastes meshed. It seemed important. And interesting. So far she had not found much of anything about which they disagreed—except his lack of faith, which was huge, and ideas of what constituted a real home, she reminded herself, sobering. His life was lived on the road, and she had deep roots. That was an enormous difference, particularly since they were each convinced they'd found their special niche in life.

Mert delivered their iced teas and left again.

Julie took the opportunity to study Ryan while he stirred sugar into his glass.

Notions of making him a permanent part of her life lurked in her mind, yet she knew better than to nurture those ideas. A sure way to make him miserable would be to try to tie him down when he wanted to be free to roam. On the other hand, merely thinking about living a nomadic life without her family and her animals sounded like a terrible trial. Ryan was right when he'd suggested they enjoy each other's company but take care to avoid getting too serious.

She squeezed the lemon wedge over her iced tea, then dropped it in and poked it with her straw while she organized her tumbling thoughts.

"You were absolutely right," Julie said.

His smile was quizzical before he chuckled quietly. "Of course I was. About what?"

"Us. We should concentrate on having fun, here and now, and not worry about the future."

"I said that? Hmm. Pretty astute for a rodeo rider."

"I thought so." She took a sip from her straw. "I'm starting to wonder how hard it's going to be to say goodbye to you at the end of the month."

"We could stop hanging out together, I suppose."

"We could."

Setting aside his glass, he reached for her hand and laid his gently over it. "Is that what you want?"

All she could do was stare at the way his hand fit so perfectly over her smaller one and shake her head.

"Me, neither," Ryan said. His grip tightened for an instant before he released her and reached for his tea again. "So what are we going to do tomorrow?"

"Pack and ship fleeces, for starters," Julie said. "That is, if you don't mind. Faith helps me when she can, but it's always nice to have an extra pair of hands."

"As long as you don't try to pull the wool over my eyes," Ryan gibed.

Julie groaned dramatically. "That was a terrible joke."

"I know, but I'm running out of Bo Peep references."

When Julie smacked his arm, she was careful to keep her touch tender and her expression easygoing. "Enough. My family knows better than to call me that to my face."

"Hey, I learned it from your brother."

"Yes, and I gave him what-for that night, too. It would be far better for you to forget you ever heard it."

Ryan made a *tsk-tsk* sound before breaking into a face-splitting grin that made the constant twinkle in his eyes even stronger. "Afraid I can't do that, ma'am. I have a real good memory, especially for anything that strikes me funny."

"That would be me?"

"Yes, ma'am, Miss Peep. That would be you."

One realization refused to leave Julie's mind during their meal. She truly did not care what Ryan called her as long as he was smiling and had that characteristic twinkle in his eyes. The more time they spent together the less she noticed the little scar on his chin and the more she was willing to tolerate just about anything in order to be with him.

That was patently foolish, of course. She knew it as well as she knew her own name—*whatever that was.* The inane thought made her chuckle softly. She covered her mouth with her napkin to stifle the noise.

"You okay?" Ryan asked. He leaned to the side to pat her back as if she was choking.

She managed a nod and a muted "Fine" before losing control and laughing out loud.

Ryan leaned away. "What's the matter? Is there barbecue sauce on my chin?"

"No. You look great." She paused for another snicker. "I tend to be a little silly when I'm tired or nervous."

"So which is it?" he drawled, studying her.

"Stop looking at me that way."

"What way?" By this time, his wide grin had returned in force and there were tiny crinkles at the corners of his mesmerizing eyes.

Julie knew this part of their dinner conversation could easily carry them into dangerous territory. Nevertheless, she decided to speak her mind.

"Like a hungry coyote eyeing a sheep," she said, softening her comment with a smile of her own.

"Not me," Ryan insisted. He continued to study her expression, but there was no rancor in his. "I'm as mild as one of your little lambs. Ask Cowboy Dan. He trusts me."

"I know he does. That's one reason I'm not worried about spending more time with you. If Dan says you're okay then you are."

Ryan was shaking his head. "I don't know that I've ever been vetted by a dog before."

"Believe me," Julie said, "you're better off with Dan than with my father. Dad is not fond of cowboys."

"I'd gathered that from stuff you said before. Don't worry about hurting my feelings. Rodeo riders are a strange breed. We don't please a lot of girls' fathers."

"You have experience dealing with that?"

"Some. I mostly concentrate on winning competitions," he finally said. "There's not a lot of time for a social life when I'm on the road all the time." Scanning the dining room, he huffed. "This is as long as I've stayed in one place in years and it feels strange."

"In that case, I'm even more glad you're winning."

"Thanks. Just remember, I'm not used to sticking around, and cut me some slack if I get too antsy. I do have plans to make a few side trips between competitions and check out some horses a friend of mine is thinking of buying."

"I understand perfectly," she said. And she did. When anything disrupted her routine, she tended to feel unsettled until she was able to restore order.

Blotting her lips with a napkin to buy thinking time, Julie glanced at her companion. There was something in his demeanor that spoke to her heart and convinced her he was truly lonely, in spite of his claims to the contrary.

"Dan is like that, too," she finally said. "All I have to do is give him a new task and he settles right down."

"You planning to tell me to run around the pasture and herd your sheep for you?"

Julie shook her head. "Not unless you drive me crazy in the office. I really am behind in my shipping and computer updates. It's really bad for business to fail to fill orders promptly, particularly from new customers."

"Fair enough," Ryan said. "Shall I bring breakfast again tomorrow morning?"

"No. If we're going to grill those steaks, I'll need to stop at the grocery store tonight anyway. I'll pick up something for breakfast and lunch, too."

"I'm not volunteering my help to force you to feed me," he said flatly. "You know that, right?"

"I know. It will probably be Faith who does the cooking anyway." The arch of one of his eyebrows caught her attention. "What?"

Ryan shook his head. "Nothing. I hope you're not inviting your sister over because you're afraid of me, that's all."

"It's not that." Julie paused, looking for the right words to explain herself. "It's scriptural. As a Christian, it's my job to keep from giving anyone the wrong impression about my morals. I trust you completely, but not everybody who sees us together is going to be that accepting. The only way to keep others from assuming I'm sinning is to use Faith as a chaperone."

He rolled his eyes. "And I thought you were a modern woman."

"I am. I just happen to care what my personal life looks like to unbelievers. It's important."

"People like me, you mean?"

"Maybe. How long has it been since you went to church?"

"How do you know I ever did?"

"Just a hunch. So how long?"

"Since my early teens. After Kirk was killed, Mom quit going and so did I."

Pondering, Julie nodded. Something told her it was too soon to ask him to accompany her the following Sunday. She'd wait. Get to know him better. Let him trust her more.

And then what? she asked herself. *Will I have the courage to press him to go with me and take the chance he'll back off completely?*

Yes, she answered. She'd pray about it, and when the time was right, she'd count on God to show her. And to provide the right words.

Even if Ryan ultimately rode off into the sunset like the hero in an old Western movie, she was going to plant the seeds of faith while he was with her. Whether or not they took root and grew wasn't up to her, it was up to the Lord Jesus. All she'd have to do is back off and not get in His way.

That was far easier to say than to do.

Ryan caught her smiling. "What's so funny? Are you laughing at me?"

"No, no. At myself," she admitted without hesitation. "There are times when my mind gets too busy and makes me feel totally out of control."

"Maybe you need to chase sheep, too?" he gibed.

Julie wondered why it was so easy to find humor in everything when she was with Ryan. If her spirits were lifted much more, she'd want to get up and dance around the café. Now, *that* would attract plenty of attention!

"Maybe I do," she told him. "I certainly have been wired lately. I guess seeing the centennial celebration begin has energized me."

"Guess so. Any word yet on the time capsule?"

"I don't think so. Cord has been working with the sheriff's department and Dad is in such a tizzy I heard he almost bit poor Deputy Cal's head off. So far there's been no progress."

"Suspects?"

"Only the ones I already mentioned. And I doubt Ellis Cooper is that kind of man. Lilibeth Shoemaker might be behind it, though. She'd

probably need help lifting the box, so maybe whoever helped her will come forward."

"If she's guilty. What makes them suspect her?"

"Threats she made after she was defeated for
the title of Miss Jasper Gulch." Julie pulled a face.
"It probably wouldn't have hurt her pride so much
if one of her chief rivals hadn't won again this
year."

Ryan laid a hand over Julie's before he said, "If
they were *really* looking for the prettiest girl in
town, they would have chosen you."

Chapter Eleven

By the time Ryan finished helping Julie for the entire day, he was more weary than he'd have been driving his truck all the way from Jasper Gulch to the Calgary Stampede. It was too bad he'd have to miss that rodeo this summer, but he'd made his choice to stay in Montana, and his prospects were certainly looking promising.

Plus, the scenery is fantastic, he added to himself, thinking of Julie more than the majestic mountain ranges and National Park lands in the distance.

Ryan stopped himself. Was he *crazy?* Apparently, because hardly a moment went by that the pretty sheep rancher wasn't on his mind.

"I wonder what might have happened if I'd chosen to go to Calgary," he muttered.

Julie had been in the house. Carrying a salad bowl toward the table in her backyard, she had apparently overheard him. "I'm glad you came to Jasper Gulch instead," she said pleasantly.

Although her unexpected arrival gave him a start, he managed to control his reaction—or so he thought. "It is funny how things work out sometimes, isn't it?"

"If you're talking about coincidences, I don't believe in those, either." She placed the wide bowl on the table and smoothed the cloth.

"You are a strange lady, Miss Peep." Hardly were the words out of his mouth before she jammed her fists onto her hips and made a face at him.

Ryan waved her off. "Sorry, sorry. I keep forgetting."

"Oh, sure you do. Just like my rotten brothers conveniently forget whenever they want to tease me. You all get a kick out of making fun of me and my sheep. Now that you've seen my operation and worked with me to ship orders, you, of all people, should appreciate that I'm a true businesswoman."

"I never said you weren't," Ryan replied, thoroughly enjoying her temporary snit. She was always pretty. When she was fired up like this, she was a real knockout. Her hair was smoldering fire, her cheeks were a summer sunset, her eyes gleamed robin's-egg blue—and when she gazed at him the way she was now, the vision of loveliness nearly took his breath away.

He decided it would be in his best interests to distract himself. "Are the steaks defrosted? This fire's almost ready."

"Any time. I put potatoes in the microwave to start them cooking in case we didn't have time to get them done on the barbecue."

"See?" He knew he was grinning foolishly but couldn't help himself. "You know a little about cooking."

"Only because I've watched Dad and Cord cook outside a lot. Mom usually bakes the potatoes in the oven, though. Dad is famous for getting the coals too hot and blackening side dishes."

"I'm sure the salad won't be overcooked as long as you leave it on the table," he joked.

"Good to know." Julie half turned. "What kind of dressing do you want?"

"What are my choices?"

"Ranch, ranch and ranch," she said with a wry smile.

"In that case, I'll have ranch."

"Excellent choice."

Watching her head back to the house, Ryan was left shaking his head. There was something so charming about this young woman, he was repeatedly astounded. Not only was she intelligent, she had a wit sharper than anyone he'd ever encountered. Yes, she had a strong work ethic, but so did he. Those tendencies led her to labor hard on the ranch and kept him traveling, yet inside they were more alike than not.

In spite of his vow to remain uninvolved, Ryan found himself thinking of the future and wondering how serious his feelings for Julie might grow by the time he finally bid her goodbye. That notion was already bothering him some. If it kept deepening he was liable to have a lot of trouble leaving her behind.

He would do it, of course. There was no way he'd consider giving up a lucrative career for the sake of one attractive woman. Still, keeping in touch with her did have a gut-level appeal that he could not deny.

Watching her return bearing a platter with the uncooked steaks, Ryan felt an unexpected jolt of awareness. Every nerve from head to toe was tingling. His heart was racing. And when he reached out to relieve her of the platter he noticed a slight tremor in his fingers.

I'm just tired and hungry, he told himself. Sure. That was the problem. After all, it had been hours since Faith had brought over leftovers for their lunch and he was also used to eating his dinner a tad earlier.

He flopped the meat on the hot grill and heard it

start to sizzle. "Is your sister going to come back and join us?" he asked.

"I don't think so." Julie gave him a smile that practically curled his toes. "She said she'd keep an eye on you from the main house but figured since we were eating in the yard, it would be safe enough for her to go home."

"Does she have binoculars trained on me right now?"

"Probably our brother Austin's telescope," Julie quipped.

He couldn't tell from her expression if she was kidding. Not that it mattered. He wasn't planning to do anything that would warrant a visit from any of the Shaws. Actually, it was kind of nice to see how much they all cared about one another and that Julie was so willing to accept their surveillance. It spoke well of her character, although by this time he had no doubt she was a fine, upstanding lady. In contrast to most rodeo groupies, she was as innocent as one of her newborn lambs.

That thought made him grin.

Julie touched his arm lightly. "What's so funny? They do have a telescope, although they usually use it for stargazing instead of spying on somebody."

"I wasn't thinking of that anymore," Ryan admitted. He gave the steaks a poke with a long-handled fork to satisfy himself they were properly positioned, then concentrated on her. "I was thinking about you."

"Really?"

"Uh-huh. Since you don't like to be called Bo Peep, I think I have the perfect substitute nickname for you."

She arched an eyebrow as she said, "I'm afraid to ask what it is."

"Well…" He purposely drew it out to get the most reaction out of her. "I thought about how much you remind me of one of your little lambs, so I thought I'd start calling you Lambchop. Kind of endearing, don't you think?"

The initial shock on her face was followed almost immediately by laughter that was so contagious he had to join in. Pretty soon they both had tears in their eyes and Julie was swishing hers away with her hands.

"Oh, brother," she finally managed to gasp out. "I will never live that one down if anybody else hears it."

"Too personal?"

"Too *something,* all right." She sniffled and sniggered, finally grabbing a paper napkin and turning away to blow her nose. "I don't think I've laughed this much or this often in years."

To Ryan's surprise he realized the same was true of him. Being with this woman was making him happier than he'd been in longer than he could remember. Maybe ever.

And that insight troubled him deeply.

As far as Julie was concerned, the only thing wrong with their meal was that it ended too soon. She supposed the steaks were delicious, particularly since Ryan seemed to have enjoyed his, but she had trouble swallowing more than a few bites. Thankfully, her dinner companion didn't seem to notice.

"So tell me more about this centennial celebration you're involved in," Ryan said as he leaned back from the table, clearly sated.

Julie was delighted to have something to talk and think about beyond her burgeoning feelings for this itinerant cowboy.

She blotted her lips again and began. "Fourth of July and the rodeo you already know about. We're changing focus each month until December, when we'll celebrate the actual founding of Jasper Gulch."

"Go on."

Since he seemed truly interested, she warmed to her subject. "In August there's going to be an old-timers' baseball game. You'd be amazed at the famous ballplayers who've come from right around here. Some of them have agreed to come back and play for us."

"Oh? Like who?"

"Hutch Garrison, for one. He's been drafted by the Colorado Rockies."

"Impressive. Anybody else?"

"Maybe Jack McGuire."

"Who's he? I've never heard that name before."

"You wouldn't have. Poor Jack was going to turn pro after college, but an injury killed his dreams. After his mother got sick, he came home and stayed to help run the ranch."

"Too bad. What's going on in September?"

"A country fair and picnic-basket auction."

"Will you have a basket entered?"

"Considering my reputation in the kitchen, probably not," Julie said with a shy smile. "I'd probably have to pay somebody to bid on mine."

"Hey, I like PB and Js."

She giggled. "Good to know, particularly if you intend to spend much more time here. I'm running out of ideas about what to feed you."

"I'll pack myself a lunch if it gets too bad," Ryan replied, mirroring her smile. "What about October?"

"You really want to know?"

"Sure. If I happen to be in the neighborhood later in the year, I may swing by."

That was the best news she'd heard in ages. "Well, let's see. You may want to keep your distance in October because we're planning the world's largest Old Tyme Wedding, with a hundred people tying the knot at the same time."

Ryan's eyebrows shot up. "A hundred couples? That's quite a challenge."

"It's just fifty brides and fifty grooms, but you're right. It is pretty far-fetched to think we can pull it off. The biggest problem will be housing everybody who's answered the ads we posted in newspapers and on the internet. I was actually surprised at all the positive response." She paused and huffed. "Of course, we are offering a lot of free services, including a big combined reception."

"Okay, I know to keep my distance in October," Ryan teased. "How about November. Is it safe then?"

"If you like parades and banquets. That will be our homecoming month. I just hope the weather doesn't interfere. It can get pretty cold here in the winter."

"Agreed. What about Christmas?"

"Actually, it's New Year's Eve when we'll end the party with commemoration of the town's founding and the burial of a new time capsule."

"Even if you don't find the old one?"

Julie shrugged. "I can't see why not. The vault is still usable and can be moved, if necessary. All we'll need is another wooden box that fits inside the concrete one and we'll be good to go. Dad plans to include a DVD of all six months' worth of celebration. It should be fascinating in another hundred years."

Lacing his fingers behind his head and leaning farther back, Ryan said, "Then you'd better include a player for it. Chances are, the whole system will be ancient history by the time somebody digs it up."

"I'd never thought of that. Thanks. I'll suggest it to the committee."

"What about the old bridge? Are you planning to rededicate that sometime before Christmas?"

She sobered and slowly, thoughtfully, shook her head. "I doubt it. We've managed to get the promise of a grant, but we have to match it to apply it and so far that's not looking very promising. It would help if some of the old-timers weren't so dead set against it."

"Like Rusty, you mean?"

"More like my father. The whole project has divided the town into two camps, those who want the bridge and those who would just as soon let it rust away." She sighed. "Personally, I wish it had never been built in the first place."

"It was probably necessary in the old days. What do your historical records say?"

"If they were properly organized I might be able to tell you. Unfortunately, they aren't. What we need is a pro to sort them. I've talked to a newcomer who's here doing research for her master's thesis."

"You mean that museum historian you said was coming back to town soon? The one who used to live here?"

"Olivia Franklin? No. A different expert. Robin Frazier is here poking through our archives for her thesis. She told me she'd try to sort out a few things for us while she's working on her own project, but I'm not holding my breath."

"Does this Robin have ties to Jasper Gulch, too?"

"Not that I know of. We don't have any Fraziers in the town's past."

"Well, maybe she'll be of help anyway. It gives you two people with research expertise."

"That's what I'm hoping for, at least until the museum project gets off the ground. The committee has settled on a location on River Road, this side of the old bridge. That's a start."

Julie pushed back from the table. "Enough about Jasper Gulch. I bought ice cream for dessert. Would you like some now?"

"Only if it's cherry vanilla," Ryan said, rising and starting to stack their plates and bowls.

Julie gaped. "I don't believe this."

"What? That I'm clearing the table for you?"

"No. The flavor of ice cream you like. I bought

three other kinds, hoping to please you, but all I usually have on hand for myself is cherry vanilla."

"Great minds think alike," he quipped, but she could tell her confession was bothering him. Truth to tell, it unsettled her, too. For two people who hardly knew each other, they were turning out to be awfully in tune.

"Next thing you know, we'll be agreeing on music," she told him. "What's your favorite song?"

His grin broadened. He stood very still, balancing the plates and looking totally serious as he said, "Hmm. That would have to be 'Baa Baa Black Sheep.'"

If he hadn't had his hands full, Julie might have slapped his shoulder playfully. Since he was holding her best dishes, she made a silly face and rolled her eyes instead.

One thing was patently clear. She and this cowboy were alike in many ways, including their desire to remain independent and their shared sense of humor. She could not recall one previous conversation in which they had remained solemn. Not one. There was always joking and laughter involved. No matter how their discussions began, they always seemed to end on a high note.

It did occur to her to wonder about Ryan's choice to avoid getting too serious. She was of like mind. Whenever life delivered problems, she looked for the good in them. That reaction was scriptural, but since Ryan wasn't a believer, it didn't explain why he did the same.

Chances were his joking was a means of covering his emotions and diverting attention from his real, tender feelings. She understood his desire to do so, particularly since he'd revealed the loss of his only brother at such an impressionable age. Nevertheless, if he was holding on to that grief instead of dealing with it, as she suspected, it was not healthy.

Why should she care what was in his heart? she asked herself. The answer was plain. Because anyone who was hurting needed to be helped, soothed, to experience the kind of unconditional love God bestowed upon His children.

Letting Ryan lead the way into the kitchen and waiting until he'd put the plates down, Julie carried the leftover salad to the refrigerator and stood with her back to him when she said, "There's a service at my church, Mountainview Church of the Savior, every Wednesday night at six. Let's plan on eating out afterward, okay?"

Dead silence behind her caused her to wonder if Ryan was still there. He was. And his expression reflected wariness.

Julie forced a smile. "What? You know I go to church all the time."

"I don't."

"Would it kill you?"

"It might."

To her relief, a lopsided smile was tugging at one corner of his mouth.

"Are you brave enough to chance it?" she pressed. "I understand they've reinforced the roof supports at Mountainview so the place probably won't collapse just because you're there."

"Is that so?"

"Not really," Julie replied. "However, as I told you, the new pastor is a younger man and not quite so traditional, although he does wear a clerical collar for Sunday services and some other duties."

Ryan shrugged and began scraping the plates. "Okay. I guess it won't be too bad. But I don't guarantee I'll know what's going on."

"I'll guide you through if you get lost," she said, beginning to picture her Australian shepherd corralling sheep. "Save what's left of my steak for Dan, will you?"

"Are you trying to change the subject?"

Although that had not been her aim, she chose to agree. "Hey, you already said you'd go with me, so there's no need to keep talking about church. I don't want you to change your mind, and Dan really does get all my good table scraps."

"There's enough steak left on your plate to feed a grown man," Ryan commented. "Are you sure you want to give it all to the one dog? What about the others?"

"They stay with the sheep 24/7 and I feed them quite well, even if they do miss a few treats." Julie glanced from the sink to the wiggling gray-and-white dog at her feet. Dan had been watching the plates until Ryan had set them on the kitchen counter, then he'd switched his attention back to her.

She laughed lightly. "Look at him, Ryan. If we're not going to at least give him some trimmings, you're going to have to be the one to break the bad news."

"He is about to jump out of his skin, isn't he? Don't tell me he's that spoiled."

"Oh, no. Not *my* dog. I'm always the boss in this house."

As she watched Ryan trim the remaining edges off the piece of delectable meat and toss them to Dan, it warmed her heart. The wise dog had temporarily transferred his allegiance to the cowboy and was getting exactly what he wanted as a reward.

So what am I supposed to learn from that? If God intended for her to kowtow to Ryan, or any man, that was *so* not going to happen. She didn't care how fond she was of her new friend, there was no way she'd defer to him. Not in a million years.

Never mind a million years, how about later this month? her thoughts countered. *Will you be*

ready to let him just ride off into the sunset with-
out speaking up?

Julie's mind said yes. Her heart was not nearly
so sure.

Chapter Twelve

If someone had told Ryan he'd end up attending the biggest church in town soon after arriving in Jasper Gulch, he'd have insisted it was impossible. Now that he was about to, he still could hardly believe it—and he'd almost missed his chance due to a small fire at the fairgrounds. By the time firefighters had put out a smoldering toolshed and had declared the incident nothing but simple vandalism, he'd had little time to shower, shave and change before heading for church.

He and Julie had not spent this particular day together, as in the past and he actually missed her. A lot. Whether or not she had planned it that way, he was so eager to see her again there was no way he was going to skip meeting her, even if he had to go to church.

When he pulled up in front and saw the place, he realized how well the building fit the country atmosphere of Jasper Gulch. The rectangular center section was built of wide planks, stacked like a log cabin, with a weathered, dark patina that complemented the rock vestibule at the very front. The steeple was white, as was the front door, which stood open at the moment.

Ryan eased his pickup into the dry-dirt lot, taking care to stir up as little dust as possible. There was Julie's truck! And there she was, too, standing on the plank walkway and shading her eyes, hopefully looking for him. For the first time since they'd met she wasn't wearing jeans, and although her skirt was long he could see her feet and ankles. She was wearing dressy sandals and a lacy knit vest over a short-sleeved top that really set off her auburn hair and fair complexion.

His heart instantly responded the way it did when the chutes opened and he was catapulted into the rodeo arena. It sped so fast he could feel his galloping pulse without trying.

There were no close spaces open, so Ryan chose one farther out, parked and jogged to Julie.

"Hi! Am I late? There was a fire at the fairgrounds and I got delayed."

"A fire? Is everybody okay?"

"Fine. No livestock was in danger, either. It looked as if kids might have been hiding in a toolshed to smoke or maybe just wanted to cause trouble. The fire department put the fire out fast."

"That's a relief. I hadn't heard a thing yet, and by the time the rumors reach me they'll probably say it was a lot worse."

She eyed his Stetson. "It would probably be easier to leave your hat outside instead of holding it during the service. My truck is closer. Just toss it in there."

"Okay. Sorry. I told you I wasn't used to going to church."

"No problem. Every cowboy needs a hat like that. Just not in church. You'd have remembered. You always took it off in the house."

"True." He managed to tear his gaze from her laughing eyes long enough to look around. "How old is this building anyway?"

"Old. It was the first church built in Jasper Gulch." Julie pointed toward a section in the rear that formed a T with the main sanctuary. "We added those Sunday-school rooms and a meeting room much later and tried to match the wood, but this part in the middle is original."

"Impressive. Those planks look hand sawed."

"I don't doubt that they weren't milled professionally like the newer ones in the back. The windows were changed from plain glass to colored sometime later, too. I love them. When the lights are on, the whole church seems to glow, and when you look from inside, the sun brings out tiny red-and-green flecks in the overall golden color."

"It is unusual. Why do they call it Mountainview?"

"Because of the view of the mountains."

"You'd still think it would be called Jasper Gulch something." He fell into step beside her. "Of course, nothing in this town is exactly the way I'd expected."

She took his arm as they walked together toward the main entrance. "Really? How so?"

Ryan merely shook his head rather than admit he was still trying to figure things out. From the very first time he'd laid eyes on Julie, he'd felt as off-balance as one of those kids hanging on to the back of a running sheep at the rodeo. His hold was slipping. He sensed a fall coming. Yet he didn't know how he'd gotten so unbalanced in a few short days. It didn't make sense. Nothing did. Not his past or his present, let alone the future he'd believed was well planned and secure.

And here he was, about to enter a church for the first time since Kirk's funeral. The notion gave him the willies. Only the woman beside him kept him from turning on his heel and walking away to protect himself from further pain.

As if sensing his unrest, Julie raised her other hand and clasped her fingers together around his elbow. "Relax," she urged with a sweet smile that reached all the way to his heart and gave it an additional jolt.

Ryan forced a grin. "Hey, I'm relaxed. It's just that we're attracting as much attention as we would if we were wearing clown makeup like the bullfighters."

She laughed. "Probably. Most people aren't used to seeing me with anybody."

"Particularly not a cowboy, I take it."

"Yup. That's part of the problem. The other is that my family worships here, too, and I think a lot of folks are waiting to see what else Dad does when he sees us together again. I heard he got pretty steamed at the fireworks show and was still upset during the rodeo that weekend."

"Should I be worried about a confrontation?"

"If Dad steps out of line tonight, I'll defend you. He tends to forget I'm all grown up and I choose my own friends."

"We are, aren't we?" Ryan said aside. "Friends, I mean. Not just pretending to be for the sake of needling your father."

"You betcha, and I'm sorry about talking you into playing games with Dad's temper. It was wrong of me."

"Guilty conscience?"

"Yes," Julie admitted. Her grin broadened and her eyes twinkled. "It's like I told my sister, my dog took to you right away and any guy Cowboy Dan likes is okay in my book."

"I bribed him," Ryan reminded her with a wink, knowing that response would bring another of the pleasing laughs he could never get enough of.

Julie did chuckle but kept it soft and barely audible. "You're going to have to stop teasing me when we get inside. I haven't gotten the giggles in church since I was a teenager and I don't want to start again now."

"Wow. Five whole years of behaving yourself? That must have been a terrible trial."

"I managed. Sort of." She schooled her features as they stepped through the open door together.

While Julie greeted others they were passing, Ryan nodded politely and tried to look a lot more relaxed than he felt as he took in the scene. The entrance to the main sanctuary was wider than the outer door to the vestibule and was standing open as if silently beckoning him, perhaps even daring him to enter.

Once they stepped through and he could see the polished pine walls of the interior, he realized what Julie meant when she'd said the colored windows glowed. Sunlight from the west, filtered by the mottled-gold glass, set the entire space on fire with warmth and an out-of-the-ordinary atmosphere that electric lighting alone could not have provided.

Unable to define what he was feeling, he realized he was sensing rather than seeing something odd, something unfamiliar yet consoling.

That alone set him more and more on edge. No matter how much peace seemed to flow around, over and through him, he was not ready to let it bring comfort. Church had never done that before and it wasn't going to do it this time, either. He was happy just as he was. He didn't need religion to lean on. He didn't need anybody or anything beyond what he'd already created to please himself.

Ryan felt his breath catch, as if there was a lump in his throat that kept him from swallowing.

That's exactly what the problem is, he realized with a start. It was his own, rigid, unforgiving attitude about making a perfect life all by himself that he was no longer able to swallow.

He glanced at the pretty girl on his arm. Julie was undeniable proof that there was something very important missing. And until he'd met her, he'd been clueless.

A lock of Ryan's hair had fallen forward when he'd removed his hat and left it in her truck. It was all Julie could do to keep from reaching up to comb his hair back with her fingers. Wouldn't *that* attract attention! No doubt she and her handsome companion were already the subject of most of the gossip that morning. Touching him like that would send the local rumor mill out of control—if it wasn't already.

She huffed. It was liable to send her own emotions through the roof, too. Fortunately, however, it was not out of the ordinary for a lady to take her escort's arm. Julie had begun doing so to pilot Ryan through the crowd at the front of the church, but by the time they'd reached an empty pew, she found she needed his physical support, as well.

Yes, that reaction was ridiculous. It was also unbelievably strong. The more she fought against her desire to be near him, the worse it got, as if some unidentified force was drawing them together. Did he feel it, too? she wondered. Perhaps. Would he ever admit as much? Probably not. The man was funny and witty and wonderful company most of the time, yet she sensed a side of his personality that he kept carefully under wraps.

If she were to guess, she'd attribute a lot of that reticence to his past, especially regarding the loss of his only brother. She didn't know what she'd be like if she'd lost even one of her siblings—and she had Christ to rely on. How awful, how lost, a person must feel facing a final goodbye without any faith in eternal life!

Julie tightened her grip on his arm and he smiled down at her. "Shall we squeeze in here?" he asked.

"Fine with me. There's an old saying that you

have to get to church early to find a seat in the back pews."

"Looks like it's true."

"I know." She released her hold on his arm in order to sidestep into the pew, and scooted over to make room. When Ryan sat down with their shoulders touching, the room temperature rose. Too bad it wasn't Sunday so she'd have her bulletin to use as a fan.

"Too warm?" Ryan asked pleasantly.

"It's just stuffy in here. Probably because the air-conditioning is broken again. Happens all the time."

"Maybe you're overdressed," Ryan suggested. "I was surprised to see you wearing a vest in the summer."

"It's one I knit from my own wool," Julie explained. "I thought it would be cool enough because it's so lacy. Guess not."

"Want me to help you take it off?"

Although his offer was obviously innocent, it made her blush. "No!"

"Okay, okay." Ryan held up both hands in surrender. "I just figured you'd be more comfortable, that's all."

She leaned closer and cupped a hand around her mouth to mute her explanation to everyone but him. "It goes on over my head, so there's no way to be subtle. Okay? The last thing we need right now is to have half the people in town watching you undress me in church."

"Might give them something to talk about," he gibed, leaning so close to her ear that his warm breath tickled the fine hairs lying against her cheek.

"I have an idea they're not lacking for gossip. Did you notice how many eyes were trained on us when we came in?"

"I sure did. I was kind of surprised you didn't stop to introduce me to some of those folks."

"All in good time," she said softly. Which was liable to be at the beginning of the service if their new pastor held to tradition. How Ryan would react was more of a mystery than how the others would behave once they were formally introduced to her companion. Chances were good that more than one mother of a single woman would invite him over for a home-cooked meal.

That seemed to be what was happening to the new pastor. She'd heard poor Ethan thanking eager mamas and papas for their offers of hospitality more than once, and rumors about his eligibility were always circulating, right or wrong. She was sure the young preacher had to be practically drowning in fried chicken and apple pie.

Besides, Julie told herself, Ryan was a nomad by profession. A wanderer who had no roots by choice. A person who didn't even make time to visit his own mother when he was close by.

She knew exactly what he was like. So why was she having such a hard time convincing herself that they had no future together? It was as if part of her knew the truth and accepted it while another part of her refused to be swayed by facts. It didn't make any more sense than a flock of sheep getting spooked by a thunderstorm and racing headfirst into barbwire fencing if there was no shepherd to calm them and turn them back.

But I do have a shepherd, Julie reminded herself. "The Lord is my shepherd."

Ryan bent closer. "What?"

She shook her head so rapidly her long, wavy curls swayed. "Nothing. I was just thinking."

"Is that allowed in church?" he quipped, looking pleased with himself.

"It is if you're quoting the Bible." She gestured toward the front of the sanctuary. "Pastor Ethan will lead an opening prayer, then take requests from the congregation for prayer for others."

"In front of everybody?"

"Not necessarily. If some don't want to be specific, they'll just say their prayer is unspoken."

"Then why bother?"

"Because God knows their needs and expects us to ask," Julie said, sighing when she saw puzzlement on Ryan's face. She reached for his hand and laced her fingers through his before she added, "He even knows where you are right now."

"Is that supposed to be good?"

"Very good," she told him gently as the lights in the sanctuary dimmed. "A good shepherd always knows where every sheep is, even the ones who've wandered off on their own."

Ryan tried to pay attention to what was going on in the service, but his mind kept taking detours. Julie detours. Then he progressed to what was left of his original family. No telling where his father was, or if the man was even alive, and, since Ryan had never known him, he had long ago stopped wondering. His mother was another story. With Kirk gone and him on the road all the time, she had to be lonely.

I should go see her soon, he told himself. The urge to argue was strong, but the sense of rightness and duty was stronger. He would make a side trip to Bozeman before he was done in Jasper Gulch, perhaps between the second week and the third when he'd already planned to have a look at some horses for sale during his downtime.

Which I could spend with Julie instead, Ryan went on thinking. That was what he really wanted to do. They'd have other days together, of course, as long as he did well in the upcoming go-rounds and stayed in the running for the big money and titles. He'd been riding well and was relatively injury-free, so his overall chances of success looked good.

Even in the hushed sanctuary, Ryan was having trouble hearing some of the softly spoken prayer requests and, since it didn't matter because he wasn't a praying man, he figured he'd just warm the pew and enjoy Julie's company.

Then he heard the pastor say something about visitors and saw Julie stand. She was tugging on his hand. "Get up."

"Why?"

"So I can properly introduce you."

"Nobody said anything about standing up in a roomful of strangers and being put on display like a market animal at the fair."

"Not to worry. I don't have a cattle prod with me." Tugging, she urged him to rise.

"I'd like you all to meet my friend Ryan Travers. He came to town for the rodeo and is ahead in points for rough stock."

"Let's all give Ryan a big Jasper Gulch welcome," Pastor Ethan urged.

Applause followed. All heads turned to look at him. Most folks were smiling, yet if Ryan could have made a run for the door without causing a scene and disappointing Julie, he'd already have been on his way out.

He saw her pivot and stare at a section to her

right. "You, too, Dad," she said, adding a chuckle to soften the command that was far from a joke.

Jackson Shaw managed a polite nod before turning to face front again.

"I don't think he likes me," Ryan whispered aside as they resumed their seats.

"He doesn't like any guys I date unless he chooses them for me," she replied.

"Is that what this is? Are we dating? Because if we are, then I'll have to make sure I don't make conflicting plans with any other local girls." An amusing flash of astonishment widened her eyes for an instant before she regained control and smiled sweetly.

"You can see whoever you want to, cowboy. Just keep in mind that I have three big brothers who look after my interests."

"Is that a threat, Lambchop?"

She covered her mouth to mute a verbal reaction, then rolled her eyes and said, "Call me that again and it just may be."

Chapter Thirteen

Julie was chagrined when she didn't hear from Ryan again after they parted company Wednesday evening. He had given her the number for his cell phone, but she hesitated to use it unless absolutely necessary.

Yes, he had seemed okay during their supper after the midweek church service, and had done well when some members of the congregation had stopped at their table to welcome Ryan during the meal, but that didn't mean he wasn't upset with her for introducing him so publicly.

Pondering the possibilities triggering his sudden silence, Julie decided to keep her distance until the upcoming Friday-night rodeo performance. There, she could casually look him up and it wouldn't seem as if she was pursuing him.

Am I? she asked herself. *Maybe. No, probably.* But to what end? She already knew how well they related to each other on a personal level, which left only their divergent lifestyles and the way they viewed Christian faith to cause conflict. Those were not small problems. If she urged him to stop competing and settle down and he ended up doing so, there was an excellent chance that he'd come to hate her for robbing him of the career he loved. On the other hand, she wasn't about to sell her sheep and hit the road for his sake either, even if there was a fair chance that the Lord had arranged their meeting. Not that their relationship had progressed nearly far enough to consider it permanent. Yet.

Julie knew that the smartest thing she could do was write him off the way she did the men her dad picked for her. Only, Ryan was different. Him she wanted around, or so she thought. Was her imagination running away with her?

The notion of stopping at the main house and having a chat with her mother, Nadine, didn't appeal nearly as much as talking with Faith or Hannah. Unfortunately, neither of them answered when she texted, so she hopped in her truck with her Australian shepherd riding shotgun and headed for town.

Hannah would definitely be at city hall because she'd been hired full-time while the centennial celebration was in progress. The single mom hated to be away from her twins all day, but she really needed the money, so she'd gratefully accepted the position.

Colorful banners announcing the rodeo as well as the overall gala still spanned the two main streets. There were additional, smaller signs on Massey Street, River Road and Mountain View, not far from the church. Right now the traffic wasn't too bad, but Julie figured the streets would be jammed again soon because of the second weekend of rodeo competition.

She parked her truck on Main and headed for city hall to find Hannah. One of the strangest things about the way she felt was her upset stomach, not to mention the fluttering of her pulse and tremors in her fingers. Hannah was her best friend. Getting together with her would surely help. Something had better.

The chamber of commerce and city hall shared the impressive old bank building in the very center of Jasper Gulch. Built of brick and stone with marble floors in the lobby and a high ceiling sporting pressed-tin tiles painted white, the edifice was more than luxurious. It echoed the glory days of Jasper Gulch, when the Shaw and Massey families had shared grandiose plans and lived the lives of land barons.

The story of what had brought down the bank and nearly killed the whole town was not one her father told often. Julie had managed to glean enough details over the years to tell that the two families had had a falling-out that had led to plenty of hard feelings and a breakup of their joint business dealings. When she was a child, there had even been a campaign to permanently change the name of Massey Street. It had failed by a slim margin when a vote was taken, but it demonstrated that her dad wasn't the only one who was holding a generations-long grudge.

Julie smiled greetings as she entered through the ornately etched glass doors and came face-to-face with her dearest friend.

"Hello, there," Hannah said brightly. "What brings you into town? I expected you to show up for the rodeo but not before."

"I needed somebody to talk to," Julie said quietly. "Have you got a minute?"

"Judging by the look on your face, this will take longer than a minute," the young mother said. "It's almost time for my afternoon break. Let me go tell the others what I'm doing and we can step outside."

On tenterhooks, Julie fidgeted while her friend ducked into one of the offices that had previously belonged to bank officials. Fortunately, the mayor was not in town today and wouldn't get curious about her visit—unless the town grapevine beat her back to the ranch.

Stepping back outside with Hannah, Julie

paused. "Let me buy you ice cream or a cup of coffee at the café?"

"Ice cream sounds good." Hannah fell into step beside her. "So what's going on? Did you have a fight with your favorite cowboy? I heard all about you taking him to church with you last night."

"That figures." Julie pulled a face and rolled her eyes. "So what did the gossip say?"

Hannah giggled softly. "Plenty. If looks could kill, the glare your father gave Ryan would have planted him six feet under. Everybody says you looked positively radiant in spite of it."

"More likely I was just really nervous," she countered. "I never dreamed he'd agree to go with me—or that Dad would show so much animosity in public."

"Is he still on the warpath? Is that what brought you to town today?"

"No. It's Ryan. He hasn't called me."

"And you don't like being ignored?"

"Something like that." They had reached the door to the small ice-cream parlor. Julie pushed through and spoke to the blonde teenager standing behind the glass shielding the tubs of ice cream. "Hi, Lilibeth. I'm buying. Give Hannah whatever she wants."

"You have to join me," Hannah insisted. "I'm not going to get fat all by myself."

"You'll never be fat." Julie wasn't hungry but

decided on a scoop of cherry vanilla in a cup so she'd have something to occupy her hands while they chatted.

Once they were seated at a small glass-topped cabaret table, Julie held up her cup and spoon. "See this? It's Ryan's favorite flavor, too."

"So?"

"So it's just one of a hundred things we have in common."

"And that's bad because…?"

Julie heaved a noisy sigh. "I don't know. It just seems really strange that we're so in tune. Know what I mean?"

"Not really." Hannah put down her spoon and leaned her elbows on the table to concentrate on her friend. "Maybe you'd better spell it out for me."

"That's the trouble," Julie said with a shake of her head and another deep breath. "I don't know what's going on or how to feel about it. Sometimes I think God brought Ryan and me together so I could help him, and other times all I see is stars and romance."

"And that frightens you."

Julie's eyes widened. "Yes!"

"Perfectly understandable. I remember being gaga over David when we were dating. He was all I could think about, all that mattered to me."

"I'm not quite that bad—yet," Julie admitted.

"But I'm certainly not my usual sensible self. I keep wondering what I should do, how I should act around him. Stuff like that never bothered me before."

"That's because other guys weren't important to you." Hannah took a spoonful and paused until she'd savored it. "If you're asking for my advice, I'd say you need to step back and slow down."

"But—Ryan's only going to be in Jasper Gulch for a little while longer. After the rodeo's over he's bound to go back on the road."

"Let him."

That was not what Julie had expected to hear. "You didn't let David go like that."

There was a glint of extra moisture in Hannah's eyes before she lowered her gaze to her cup of ice cream and nodded. "I know. I panicked and talked myself into getting married in a hurry when I probably should have waited."

"You were madly in love, right?"

"Oh, yes. That's not what I'm trying to say. It's just that sometimes, when I look at the twins and think about raising them all alone, I wonder if it wasn't a mistake to rush into getting married before David shipped out. If I'd known then what I know now..."

Julie reached across the tiny table and patted the back of her friend's hand. "But you didn't know.

And if you hadn't taken a chance, you wouldn't have such beautiful reminders of your husband."

"I know. I do love those two babies. But I wanted to curl up and die when I was giving birth and already knew they'd never see their daddy or get to know the wonderful man he was. An event that should have been filled with joy was bittersweet instead." She raised her misty gaze to Julie. "What I'm trying to say is, don't be in a hurry to commit to Ryan—or to any man. If God brought you together, He'll finish what He started. If not, then it wasn't meant to be."

Nodding soberly, Julie said, "Okay, I guess. It's going to be hard to back away, though. In the short time I've known him, I've discovered how much we have in common. Letting him go away without telling him how I feel seems unfair."

When Hannah looked at her and asked, "Unfair to which one of you?" Julie was momentarily rendered speechless. Her friend was absolutely right.

"I get it," Julie finally replied. "If I fall all over myself convincing Ryan we belong together, it could turn out to be much harder for him."

"Exactly. If you truly do care about his feelings, you need to let him make the decision to stay or go without undue influence. And if he's the man you think he is and he cares for you, he'll make the right decision in the long run. If not, you haven't really lost a thing except some pipe dreams."

"Suppose he walks away and never looks back?" The mere words battered Julie's tender heart, although she knew they were sensible.

"Then you'll have your answer," Hannah said softly. "If he leaves you without confessing love, you'll be sure your romance is one-sided."

"I never said I loved him," Julie said softly.

Hannah met her misty gaze. "You didn't have to. I've known you too long to fail to notice the signs."

Ryan figured he'd checked his cell for missed calls at least once an hour for the past forty-eight. In view of the fact that Julie had his number and had not returned his call, he figured she must have had enough of his company. That conclusion didn't sit well, but he was forced to accept it. And, since the next weekend of competition was about to begin, he assumed she'd be in the stands. At least that was something to look forward to.

His bareback bronc was new to him. She was a bony, rangy animal the size of a small bucking bull and refused to stand still in the chute while he tried to tighten his rigging.

"Get ready to pull 'er tight when I poke her in the flank," the stock contractor said. "She likes to suck air and blow herself up so your cinch'll slip."

"Okay. Thanks."

Ryan had no choice but to concentrate on the

wily horse if he hoped to stay on her back for the full eight seconds. Although he hadn't forgotten to scan the grandstands for Julie, he needed to take care of business right now.

The bronc's mane was roached, cut short and bristly, except for a long forelock, and there were leftover signs of a winter coat on her cheeks and chin, making her look as though she needed a shave. If Ryan hadn't been preparing to ride, he might have found the stray longer hairs on the bay amusing.

Stepping across the narrow chute, Ryan placed one boot on either side and straddled the animal before easing onto her back. He could smell the horse's sweat, see her wild eyes rolling back as she tried to turn and look at him. Crossties on a halter kept her head from swiveling much, and that seemed to agitate the bay even more.

It didn't help that some idiot holding a large camera and wearing headphones kept leaning in over the front of the last chute and spooking the bronc. *Television.* The equipment for recording his previous rides did enable him to critique them, but right now it was mostly distracting, not to mention frightening, to the already fractious horse.

He took one last quick peek at the grandstand, wedged his rosined glove into the rigging and settled onto the animal's twitching hide.

She gathered herself beneath him. Ready. Anxious. Snorting and tossing her head as much as she could while restrained.

Ryan nodded.

The wranglers let go of the ropes.

The gate latch clicked, setting everything in motion.

The horse reared, poised for her first leap. She exploded out of the chute, nearly knocking the gate man down as she rushed past.

Ryan gritted his teeth, glad he was using a football player's mouth guard, particularly when she landed flatfooted and jarred him all the way to the marrow of his bones.

He raked her withers in rhythm with her leaps. The smooth rowels on his spurs didn't hurt her, they merely allowed him to keep his balance and put on a good show, as well as earn more points for his ride.

This was the moment when he always wondered when or if the horn was ever going to blow. Eight seconds became an incalculable span of time.

His fingers were working loose in spite of being wedged into his rigging. Ryan tried to tighten his grip. One more jump. Just one more jump....

Suddenly, he was airborne. And the hard dirt floor of the arena was a long way down.

He heard the horn sounding as he was flying through the air. It stopped before he actually landed. Had he made it? Was the ride going to count?

The side of his head slammed into the ground. That was the last thing he remembered.

Julie was on her feet. So were most of the other spectators. Cheers turned to screams and shouts. Medics who had been standing by rushed into the arena. Flashing lights on a waiting ambulance began to rotate.

Breath held, Julie had watched Ryan hit the dirt in a cloud of dust and just lie there. So still. So deathly quiet. Mere moments passed until he was surrounded by rescuers and hidden from her view.

Success of the ride was nothing compared to his well-being. She strained to see if he was moving. It was impossible to tell. In no frame of mind to linger or wait until the crowd cleared the arena floor, Julie bounded down the stairs between the banks of bench seats, hitting the ground running.

Riders blocked her path to the alley leading to the gates. "Excuse me? Please?"

"You can't go in there," one of the burly steer wrestlers said.

"But I have to."

His extended arms kept her back. "Let the pros do their jobs. That's what they're here for."

"I know, but…" Spotting Carrie Landry among the medical team, she bounced on her toes and waved. "Carrie!"

The other woman waved a gloved hand and

made an okay sign in reply. Julie was instantly relieved, so much so that she felt weak in the knees.

A few more anxious seconds passed before she saw Ryan's mussed hair above the heads of the others. "Thank God," she whispered to herself. More prayer and thanksgiving was in order, but at the moment she was barely able to think, let alone offer a proper prayer.

Ryan was moving now, acting as if he might be sore from the hard landing but mobile. And when she saw his face, he was grinning from ear to ear.

She was already heading for him when he reached the back of the chutes. "Hey!" She waved an arm. "Great ride!"

He raised a hand in greeting, bracing himself as if he thought her speedy approach meant she was planning to throw herself at him. The idea did occur to her. Fortunately, she was able to put the brakes on her enthusiasm and her feet at the same time.

"I wondered if you'd be here," he said, clearly glad to see her.

"Wouldn't have missed it for the world," Julie replied. "You ride really well. I'm not quite as sure about your get-offs, though."

"The ground always manages to be there when I land," he quipped. "I've never missed it."

"Good to know. How about waiting for the pickup men the next time? It's a lot easier on the spectators when you don't fly through the air like a wounded duck."

His rich laugh sent tingles all the way to her fingertips.

"Believe me, that dismount was not in my plans." Ryan gestured toward the rear where his rigging was waiting, and she fell into step beside him. "I sort of pictured myself as a flying super-hero, not a duck," he said. "You really know how to give compliments."

"Hey, you called me Lambchop, remember?"

"Touché. So did Faith come with you today?"

"Not this time. She's rehearsing for a concert." Julie couldn't help being so elated she was almost giddy. "I can't imagine anybody putting violin music ahead of watching a live rodeo."

"Not unless you call it a fiddle and play in a country-and-western band," he countered. "That's altogether different."

"She can play that way when she wants to," Julie said. "She just prefers classical music."

"To each his own." Ryan picked up his bare-back rigging, thanked the wrangler who'd handed it to him then turned back to her. "Walk with me while I stow this and get my saddle and halter?"

"Sure. I didn't notice what your score was this time, did you?"

"High eighties, I imagine. I can usually guess about where I'll place, given a clean mark-out and a decent horse. It's the final totals that matter the most anyway."

"I'm glad to see you're okay." She had to hurry to keep up with his long, purposeful strides.

"I'd have to hit a lot harder than that to stay down," Ryan told her, sobering. "We can never tell, though. Sometimes even a clean get-off can mean a twisted ankle or getting kicked. Take that horse I rode last weekend, for instance. She was ready to run over anything in the arena, particularly me."

Without thinking, Julie slipped her hand through the bend in his elbow and grasped his arm. "I remember." What she wanted to do was continue to express her concern and urge him to shun danger. She didn't. She knew better than to interfere in his life choices or let herself sound as if she didn't trust his judgment.

I don't trust it, she told herself with a shy smile and an averted gaze. Yes, she found rodeo thrilling. Exciting. Pure joy and a rush of adrenaline. Yet she also sensed that she was developing an aversion to the situations in which a rider deliberately put himself in jeopardy. Every time Ryan entered the arena and risked life and limb, the sensation grew until she was beginning to wish she'd stayed home.

Her grip tightened and she could feel the strength of his arm, the flexing of his muscles.

This man was as capable and professional as anybody she'd ever met, yet there was no way he could guarantee that his career would not cripple or kill him. No one could. There were inherent dangers even for the ropers and steer wrestlers, not to mention the occasional judge or gate man who got run over by a rampaging bull.

They reached Ryan's truck. After exchanging his bareback rigging for the equipment he'd need for saddle-bronc riding, he caught Julie's eye. "A penny for your thoughts?"

"You'll laugh."

"Possibly. Probably. I think I've laughed more since you and I met than I have in the ten years prior.

"Okay." She huffed and began to shake her head. "I was just picturing how much safer being a rodeo cowboy would be if everybody substituted sheep for horses and cattle."

When he started to chortle as though he was choking, she patted him on the back. "See? I warned you."

"Yes…you did," Ryan said, coughing. "I'd have been fine if I hadn't pictured it."

Julie was laughing now, too. "I know. And instead of cowboy I'd have to call you sheepboy. That just seems really wrong, doesn't it?"

Shock replaced his grin for a split second before

he started laughing so hard he sagged against the truck and swiped at his eyes.

Finally, he recovered self-control enough to say, "You are one of a kind, Lambchop. Do you know that?"

"It may have come up in conversation a time or two," Julie replied. "Mostly when I was a kid and my older brothers and sister tried to get me into trouble."

"They didn't often succeed, did they?"

"Uh-uh. I was too little and too innocent looking. Mom and Dad usually ended up scolding the others for picking on me. That worked until... Well, I guess it kind of still does."

Ryan sobered slightly. "You really are fortunate to have such close siblings."

"I know. I promised to meet them later this evening so I'd better go."

Julie sent an empathetic smile his way, hoping and praying he would understand when she added, "They're all a special blessing from God."

She paused for effect before adding, "So are you."

Chapter Fourteen

Final saddle-bronc scores were close. Two men were tied for second and there were only fractions of points separating them from the leader—Ryan Travers.

His former rodeo coach had always said that the rider who wasn't a little bit afraid was in trouble. Ryan had never truly understood that viewpoint until today. Not only was he feeling uneasy about his upcoming bull rides, he thought he'd figured out why, and he didn't like his conclusions one bit.

Before coming to Jasper Gulch, he had ridden as if he didn't care whether or not he was injured—because he didn't. It was as if his life wasn't worth the worry. Oh, he always rode to win. That was a given. But he wasted little thought on whether or not he made it to the eight-second whistle in one piece.

And then he'd met Julie. She'd made him care

too much, and it was ruining his confidence, undermining the bravado he counted on. Even if he managed to temporarily put her out of his mind, the change in attitude lingered. He wanted to live. To be happy. To…

"To what?" Ryan muttered under his breath. For a guy who prided himself on having a practically nonexistent personal life, he was sure mixed up at the moment.

He was on his way to the arena with his bull rope when he felt a tap on his shoulder. Wheeling, he frowned, wondering where he'd seen the familiar face before.

"It must be the lack of a collar," Ethan said, apparently recognizing Ryan's confusion. "I only wear it for official church business." He offered a hand. "Ethan Johnson. I had the pleasure of introducing you in church last Wednesday evening."

"Right. Sure." Ryan accepted his hand and grasped it firmly, surprised to note that the preacher was strong in his own right. "So did Julie send you?"

Ethan's puzzled expression was his answer even before the man shook his head and said, "No. Why should she?"

"Because I'm a backslider," Ryan said, starting to relax. "Hadn't been in church for years until she talked me into going with her."

"I see you didn't suffer much from associating with us. I hope we'll see you there again."

"I won't be around long enough to count as a regular," Ryan said. "Besides, God isn't interested in me."

"He's always interested," Ethan countered with a smile. "But I can relate to thinking otherwise. I wasn't always a pastor."

"Really?"

Ethan nodded soberly, his lips pressed into a thin line. "A man's past is just that—past—when he comes to the Lord and asks for forgiveness. It's a new start, a new birth, just the way baptism portrays it. You symbolically die to your old self, are buried with Jesus, then reborn as one of His children. Simple."

"Not for me."

"How long have you been fighting God?"

Ryan's jaw gaped. He snapped it shut. "I don't know what you're talking about. Are you sure Julie isn't hiding somewhere watching us?"

"Nope. I haven't seen her. But I can see pain in your eyes. The only really sad part is that you don't have to suffer. Forgiveness is only a prayer away."

"Like I said before, not for me," Ryan insisted.

Ethan clapped him on the shoulder. "If you should happen to change your mind, I'm always available to talk. Just stop by the church or give me a call. The number for the office is in the phone book, and here's my card with my cell number."

Although Ryan accepted the pastor's business card because it was the polite thing to do, he had no intention of using it. Nor was he planning to attend church again. It was too stressful, made him think too much, remember too much. Some parts of the past were best put out of a man's mind and kept there. Dwelling on his mistakes wouldn't bring back his brother. Nothing would. Kirk was gone and it was his fault for keeping silent when he should have spoken up and told their mother what had been going on. If only he hadn't promised....

"Listen, kid, you break your word and tell Mom, I'll wail on you, you hear," Kirk had warned. "If she cared whether or not I had a few drinks with my buddies she'd stay home more."

"But Kirk...those guys are trouble. You said so yourself."

"Only to keep you out of trouble, little brother. I'll be back before Mom misses me. She's working late tonight. Remember? She said so."

Young Ryan had bit back worry and frustration. "Then take me with you."

His older brother's laugh had been loud, hoarse. "Oh, sure. That would do my rep a lot of good.

You'd have to sit in the car anyway. You're way too young for bars."

"So are you!" Ryan remembered shouting.

His fists clenched again and he heard Kirk's cynical laugh as the memory strengthened. That was the last time he'd spoken to his brother, the last time he'd seen him alive.

Their mother had come home from work to find Ryan curled up on the sofa, sniffling, while a couple of uniformed police officers waited to break the bad news to her.

Ryan had known there had been a disaster the moment they'd knocked on the door. By that time it was too late to tell and save Kirk's life. Too late to do anything except blame himself.

He still did. Guilt was only wrong if you had no sins to atone for. There were plenty of other mistakes in his life, yes, but nothing compared with the loss of his only brother. Absolutely nothing.

Julie's seat with her family was first-class and much more comfortable than the regular bleachers. The only drawback was her inability to quickly jump down and mingle with the cowboys after Ryan's upcoming bull ride.

She noted Adam looking past her and followed his sidelong glance to their father. Jackson Shaw was pouting like an unhappy little boy while closely studying her.

"What's the matter, Dad? I'm here, aren't I?"

"You clearly don't want to be. What's come over you, Julie? You used to be such a sensible, obedient child."

Her smile was punctuated by Adam's cough and chuckles from Cord and Austin. "I think the boys might disagree," she said. "Being the youngest wasn't all bad. I got away with a lot more than the others did."

Jackson bristled. "Are you saying your mother and I didn't do a good job raising you?"

Julie's gaze met Nadine's and lingered, then drifted back to her dad. "You were both great parents," she said. "I was a little stinker part of the time, that's all. Every kid goes through a rebellious period."

"I never saw that in you," Nadine said, grasping her husband's large hand.

"That's because she saved it all for now," Jackson argued. "If you think I'm going to put up with you chasing all over the country after a no-good cowboy, you have another think coming. Remember who owns the ranch."

"You gave me the piece I'm living on for my twenty-first birthday." The anger he was displaying gave her the shakes and made her wonder what else he was going to threaten to do to control her.

"The acres around your house. Not all that pasture land you're using."

"Now, Jackson…"

Julie saw the discomfort in her mother's expression, sensed it in her halfhearted plea to her father for compassion.

Rendered speechless, Julie diverted her attention to the arena, set her jaw and clasped her hands in her lap. Her own father had just threatened to force her to thin her flock and perhaps give up her entire business. He had always been totally supportive. Would he go back on all his promises simply to get better control of her and keep her away from Ryan?

The whole concept was ridiculous. She loved her father as much as she loved the rest of her family. How could he be so cruel in return? If he was truly serious and not just throwing out baseless threats, she was going to have to question her judgment regarding everyone and everything.

Public-address broadcasts that echoed across the arena came from the announcer's stand directly behind her, so she heard the words twice with a split-second delay. It was Ryan's turn to ride. She perched on the edge of her chair, barely breathing, and wondering if her family was watching the action at the chutes or her reaction to it.

She tensed. Clasped her already tingling fingers so tightly they throbbed. Saw Ryan nod, ride skillfully and safely dismount. This time.

Her pounding heart felt as if it were lodged in

her throat. Unshed tears misted her vision. If she left the mayor's special booth and went to Ryan now, it could cost her everything. If she didn't, she'd be ceding her pride and freedom to unfair threats and one man's power trip. The Jackson Shaw who had raised her was not a vindictive person, he was simply a stubborn man who was used to being in charge and found it difficult to back down, even when he was wrong. And *she* was every bit his daughter.

Rising, Julie calmly approached her father. "For the record, Dad, Ryan and I started out pretending to be a couple, just for fun. But now I can see that it's time to rethink that status."

She bent and gave her father a quick kiss on the cheek. Then she stood tall, turned and walked off the platform.

Ryan had already reclaimed his gear and was talking to a group of fellow competitors when he spotted Julie in the distance.

One of the other men slapped him on the back. "Look sharp, Travers. Here comes your fan club."

A shorter rider guffawed. "Yep. The president and only member. To look at you two, a fella might think you were getting serious."

"Not me," Ryan insisted, feeling his gut twist in disagreement.

"In that case," the first man said, spitting aside

into the dirt, "maybe I'll see if she'd like to have supper with me instead of you."

The group chuckled and hooted derisively when Ryan lifted his chin and said, "Over my dead body."

"That's what we thought," someone else commented. "So what're you waiting for? Go get 'er, cowboy."

Pausing only long enough to shoot them a warning look and declare, "Cool it," Ryan turned and hurried toward Julie.

The closer he got, the stronger became the urge to open his arms and invite a hug. Would she permit it? She seemed to be matching his enthusiasm, but did he really want to take their friendship to another level?

"I am totally out of my mind," he muttered, slowing so she could take the final few steps and choose how close they ended up. It was close. Very close.

When she finally halted, breathless and flushed, she didn't speak.

Neither did Ryan.

They gazed into each other's eyes and just stood there, silent, waiting.

Ryan could hear whistles and catcalls coming from the cowboys he'd been with after his last ride. Did Julie hear them? Could she tell they were for her?

He gave her a lazy smile and arched his brows. "Ignore those guys. They're just jealous."

"What?" She seemed to snap out of whatever had been keeping her attention so narrowly focused.

Ryan gestured over his shoulder. "The bunch behind the chutes. They were teasing me when you got here and don't have enough sense to shut up."

"I guess I should be flattered."

"Only if you enjoy being the center of that kind of attention." He sobered, studying her. "Hey, what's wrong?"

"Nothing. It's not important."

"Anything that makes you unhappy is important." He took her arm and urged her away. "Come on. You can tell me what's bothering you while I stow my gear in the truck."

She resisted. "Really. It's nothing."

What he wanted to do was grab her shoulders, hold here still and make her face him until she confessed. Instead, he gave a nonchalant shrug. "Is there a problem with your lambs?"

"No, they're fine."

"The dogs, then? Cowboy Dan?"

"He's fine, too." Her lower lip was quivering.

That was enough to make Ryan drop his gear bag and follow his earlier instincts by cupping her shoulders. "Look at me, Julie. We haven't known each other long but I can tell when you're upset. Unless you want to wait and unload on your sister or brothers, you may as well open up to me. I have broad shoulders."

It was a shock to feel her hands starting to slip around his waist. Tears glistened in her eyes moments before she stepped closer and laid her cheek on his chest.

Ryan embraced her. What else could he do? Not only was she acting brokenhearted, his own emotions were surging, his pulse racing and jolting like the rankest bucking horse he'd ever ridden.

At this moment, in this place, in front of everybody behind the chutes and half the folks in the nearby grandstands, he could not have stepped away from this woman if he'd wanted to. And he definitely did not want to.

He gently stroked her back, feeling her shudders as she fought to regain self-control. Ryan was surprised and more than a little chagrined when she quickly recovered and raised her face to swipe away scant tears.

"Sorry," Julie said. "I'm not usually a crybaby."

"I'm sure you had good reasons."

Arching an eyebrow and managing a slight smile, she nodded. "Oh, yeah. I just can't believe my father meant what he said."

In view of past conversations, Ryan had a pretty

good idea what the problem was. "I take it he told you he doesn't like me much."

"In a manner of speaking."

"Care to elaborate?"

"Not really. My father is my worry, not yours."

"If you say so. Remember, I did agree to hang out with you to make a point with him. Sounds like we succeeded."

Julie began to smile sweetly. A little moisture lingered on her dark lashes, making her blue eyes glisten like ice crystals atop a winter snow. "Yes. You might say we overdid it a tad."

Relaxing, Ryan started to ease away from her in response to her comment. She tightened her hold on his waist and kept him close. That was confusing, given their very public position.

"In that case," he offered, "maybe we'd better not act quite so friendly."

"On the contrary," Julie said flatly. "I think it's high time I did something I've been wanting to do for ages."

"Oh?" Ryan knew he was smiling, but he couldn't help it. The grin spreading across her lovely face was an inescapable influence. So was the mischievous twinkle in her eyes—and he wasn't mistaking unshed tears for mirth. He could read this woman like a book. She was definitely up to something. Something that clearly included him.

She leaned closer.

Startled, Ryan resisted.

You could have knocked him over with a feather when she raised both hands and cupped his cheeks to hold him still, tilted her head and touched her lips to his.

The effect was instantaneous. Every nerve in his body fired as if receiving an electric shock from a cattle prod. He could barely breathe.

Then he saw her slowly close her eyes and felt her deepen their kiss.

Sighing, he counted to three before clasping her wrists and holding them tightly so he could back off.

"Julie…"

She swayed. Opened her eyes. Stared at him as if seeing him for the very first time. "Oh, wow."

"Yeah, me, too."

"Then why did you stop me?"

"A guy can only take so much, Lambchop. I know you're mad at your father, but this isn't the way to get back at him."

"I wasn't doing that."

"I'm afraid you were. I'm not saying I didn't like it, I just think it would be better to cool it until you're not furious with your dad. We'd both enjoy it more."

She fanned herself with her open hand the way she had in the overly warm church. "I don't know about you, but if I'd enjoyed that kiss much more I'd probably have fainted dead away. And I *never* faint."

"Then it's a good thing I didn't kiss you back," he gibed, hoping she'd believe him. Her wide-eyed expression and lopsided smile said otherwise.

She shook her head and drawled, "Ri-i-i-ight."

It was Ryan's turn to blush. His cheeks felt as if they were afire. "Okay. Maybe I did kiss you a little, but only because you took me by surprise."

"That's a relief. I'd hate to think that was the best you could do."

"What did you say, Lambchop?"

"Oh, nothing. Just citing my opinion."

Ryan acted before he could talk himself out of it. He grabbed her and literally swept her off her feet. Bending her over one arm while supporting her so she wouldn't fall backward, he aimed directly for her lips.

Julie's arms slipped around his neck. He felt her eager response to the kiss and it shook him so badly he had to take care not to drop her.

Passersby stopped to watch. A few applauded. The cowboys in the crowd who knew him whistled and hooted approval.

He knew he had proved his point and should end their romantic embrace immediately. It was a real struggle to act at all, let alone appear nonchalant when that kiss had just turned his world upside down.

Nevertheless, Ryan drew her upright and steadied her until he was certain she was stable, then let go and stepped away. Her eyes were enormous and misty. Her cheeks were rosy. Her lips trembled as if beckoning to him to repeat their kiss again and again and again.

Julie's hands slid across his shoulders and traced a path down each arm, ending by briefly touching his fingers.

Given another time and place, Ryan might have grasped and held her hand. Since they were already causing a scene, he chose to hoist his gear bag and doff his hat to the spectators before looking to Julie. "I think we'd better make our exit."

A grin split her face. "Probably. Where to?"

"Anyplace but here. I don't want to be around when your family hears about what just happened and comes looking for me."

"I'm shocked," she joked, one hand at her throat. "You're fearless in the arena."

"That's because all I have to face there are angry two-thousand-pound animals with bad attitudes. I don't think I could defend myself against your dad *and* your three big brothers."

"Don't worry." Julie hurried to keep up with

his long strides. "If worse comes to worst, I'll protect you."

He nodded. "It's a deal...Lambchop."

Chapter Fifteen

There wasn't one detail about Ryan's amazing kiss that Julie couldn't vividly recall. She relived the experience constantly and was still awed when they finally bid each other good-night, after coffee at a gas station quick stop, and started for their respective homes.

Home. The thought echoed in her mind as if it were bouncing off solid walls. She loved her little cottage and the life she'd made for herself. What would she do if her father actually did withdraw his support? Surely it had been his anger speaking when he'd made the threat, not his true heart. He'd always insisted he wanted each of his offspring living nearby, preferably on Shaw land, and sharing both his life and his ranch. The boys all worked for him, in one capacity or another, and even Faith put in some hours there.

Faith had her music, of course. And Cord was

involved in local politics. But all the Shaw siblings listened to what Jackson wanted and tried to comply with his wishes, even as adults. So what was wrong with her? Julie wondered. Why did she seem so intent on bucking his authority?

"Because he's wrong this time," she whispered to herself. "There's a lot more to Ryan Travers than his choice of career."

In her deepest heart she knew Ryan needed her. It wasn't a sensible conclusion, it was simply true. She knew it as well as she knew her own name. It didn't matter why he had entered her life. All she cared about was him, as a person, as a man who had been suffering and desperately needed emotional healing.

Beyond that, there were her own tender feelings, of course. She didn't intend to deny those. She had already made up her mind that Ryan came first. Once he made his peace with the Lord and with his traumatic past, she would begin to consider whether or not he should be a part of her future. However, Hannah was at least partially right. Julie might be falling head over heels for this cowboy, but she needed to back off and bide her time. *Easier said than done.*

Driving onto the ranch and pulling up in front of her cozy house, Julie spotted a figure waiting on her porch. Her pulse jumped. *Not Dad,* she prayed silently. *Please, God, don't let it be Dad.*

The comforting answer came when Nadine stood and paused at the top of the wooden steps.

Dan galloped off the porch and began to circle Julie the moment she stepped from her truck. She gave his head a pat and his ears a quick ruffle as she headed for her waiting visitor.

"Hi, Mom. Is everything okay?"

"No. We need to talk."

Shivers of anticipation and alarm shot up Julie's spine and prickled on the back of her neck. There had only been a few times in recent memory that her mother had chosen to intercede between father and offspring. The fact that she was asking for a discussion tonight did not bode well. Not well at all.

"Sure. Come on in. I'll put on a pot of decaf and it can brew while I check my email so I don't overlook any rush orders. Then we'll sit down, relax and talk."

Nadine didn't argue. Julie would have taken that as a good sign if the older woman had not started wringing her hands and pacing. "I shouldn't be here."

"Nonsense. You're my mother and this is my house. Of course you're welcome."

"You know what I mean. Your father wouldn't like it."

"Do you always follow his orders?"

"Mostly." She plopped into a chair at the kitchen

table as if someone had just shoved her into place. "Read Proverbs 31."

"The perfect-wife chapter. I know. I don't recall anything about being your husband's doormat, though."

"Your father means well. You must know that. He just has your well-being and future happiness in mind."

"Don't you think I should be the judge of that?" Julie took care to keep her voice as neutral as possible and avoid provoking more anger.

"Yes, I do," Nadine said. "And I believe he'll eventually come around if Ryan is the man you choose to marry. Just don't be foolish and rush into anything."

"I'm not. Ryan and I happen to get along really well. He makes me laugh and I do the same for him."

"There's a lot more to marriage than a few laughs."

"Don't I know it." She switched on her laptop and let it retrieve her email while she watched the slow drip of coffee into the glass pot. "Here's the thing. Ryan has no intention of settling down and I won't consider leaving all this and hitting the road, so you can tell Dad to stop worrying."

"You might change your mind."

"I might. Or Ryan might. But it doesn't look promising. There's a lot in his past that's driving him, and I'm afraid until he comes to terms with that, there's no hope for us."

"You'd like it to be otherwise." It was not a question.

Julie sighed and pressed her lips together, recalling the kiss that had begun in jest and ended all too seriously. "Yes," she said softly, contemplatively. "I would very much like it to be different."

Ryan had not been too surprised when Julie began to avoid him. After all, he had literally swept her off her feet in public. She had seemed unduly nervous in the short time they'd spent together right afterward, even though he'd done his best to tease her out of it, and now it looked as if she might be pulling even further away. Sunday was fast disappearing and he'd seen no sign of her.

"I should have known better," he muttered to himself as he gathered up his gear. "I never should have let her goad me into another kiss."

Yeah, as if you didn't want to kiss her, his conscience argued. He'd let his personal desires overwhelm logic and scare her away.

Disgusted with himself, he gritted his teeth and contemplatively shook his head. So now what? He supposed he could merely wait until she came to watch him ride again and try to catch her after each event. That was what a normal person would do. But the final rodeo weekend was five days away. Could he stand to wait that long? He doubted it.

Besides, he argued to himself, climbing into his truck, *I don't want her to stay upset for a whole week.*

That wasn't the real reason, of course. Ryan wasn't fooling himself. He knew full well that his main reason for seeking her out was that he yearned to see her again, to hear her laugh, to see the sparkle in her eyes when she smiled at him. *If she ever smiled at him again.*

Checking the time on his dashboard clock, he noticed it wasn't all that late. Julie had said she'd skipped Sunday-night services in order to watch him ride the previous weekend. Since he hadn't spotted her tonight, there was a fair chance she'd gone to church instead.

And if she is there, then what? he asked himself. *What are you going to say to her?*

I'll apologize for embarrassing her, he assured himself.

And then what?

He had no idea. None at all. He certainly wasn't in a position to get serious about her, nor was he foolish enough to suggest otherwise. Julie knew who and what he was. She'd been attracted to him because of her love of the sport of rodeo, so she already knew he was a rover by profession. Even if they did decide to conduct a long-distance romance, how long would it be before she got tired of missing him and moved on to a more stable relationship?

The notion of being away from a loved one for months at a time needled Ryan's conscience until he had to admit again that it was high time to pay his mother a visit. Yes, it was hard to do. And yes, he hurt worse after each time he saw her. But this time he'd go. This time he would muster the same kind of courage it took to step onto the back of a bucking bull and do what was right, even if facing his mother and knowing how much she blamed him for Kirk's death nearly killed him.

By this time he was passing the church. The lights were on inside. Worshippers were filing out the front door and standing in small groups, chatting or heading for the parking lot.

Ryan wheeled in, saw Julie's truck, parked nearby and forced himself to wait until she appeared.

It wasn't easy.

Julie saw her mother grab her father's arm and stop him. Following their line of sight, she immediately understood who they were staring at. Ryan was here.

Adding to Nadine's urging, Julie raised her arm to block him. "No, Dad. Just take Mom home. I want to talk to Ryan in private."

"What are you going to say that we shouldn't hear?" Jackson demanded. "After that incident I heard about at the rodeo grounds, I can just imagine."

It was all she could do to contain her rising temper. "Look, Dad, I know you only have my welfare in mind, but I'm a grown woman. I can take care of myself." Observing the rancor in his stare, she added, "And don't bother threatening to disown me or kick me off Shaw land again. You and I both know that's the last thing you want."

Julie could see his jaw muscles clenching before he nodded and heaved a noisy sigh. "Okay. Go. Just remember what I've always told you."

"There are a thousand things you've warned me about," Julie replied with a tender smile. "Trust me. I'm not planning to elope with a wandering cowboy and abandon everything I love here in Jasper Gulch."

The moment the word *elope* was out of her mouth, she rued even thinking of it. Life on the road with Ryan would be so foreign to her she'd probably weep all the time from homesickness, so why did the notion of spending every day with him continually tug at her heart?

Waving, she approached the truck he was leaning against. He made no move to go to her.

"Hi," Julie said, hoping she didn't sound half as breathless as she felt. "Is the rodeo over already?"

"Yes."

"So tell me. How did you do?"

"Okay."

"Just okay?" She started to reach for his arm, then stopped short of touching him. "Who's high-point man in rough stock now?"

"I guess I am."

"Wonderful!" Although she was excited by Ryan's success, she was puzzled by his nonchalant reporting of it. "That's good day money, too. Right?"

He merely nodded.

"Why are you here? I get the idea there's something on your mind."

"I figure I owe you an apology."

"For what?"

"That kiss in public. It got you into trouble, right?"

"Nothing I can't handle."

"Then why haven't you been watching me ride the way you were before?" He glanced over her shoulder. "Trouble with the family?"

"Actually, not much, considering," Julie said, smiling. "I chose to come to church tonight because I knew I needed it."

"Needed it how?"

"It's a long story. Too bad you didn't get here a little earlier. Pastor Ethan delivered a great sermon."

"It's not like when we went Wednesday evening?"

"No. Sunday night's service is similar, but more casual than the one on Sunday morning, except when we have communion."

"It's all Greek to me." Ryan shoved his hands into his pockets and lounged against the closed door of his truck. "I wanted to tell you I'm going to be leaving town tomorrow."

Julie could barely speak. "You—you are? I thought you said you had good scores."

"I did. I'll be back long before the last weekend's competition. I'm going to run up to Bozeman and see my mom."

Again, she started to reach for him, desperate to impart approval. "I'm so glad."

"Yeah, well, I'm not. But I'm going anyway."

"Don't you two get along at all?" It seemed improbable that anybody would fail to appreciate Ryan's uplifting presence until she compared his home situation to her own. Sometimes those who were dearest were the hardest to understand and empathize with.

"We haven't been close since Kirk died," Ryan said quietly. "I doubt we ever will be again."

This time, Julie did touch his arm briefly. "I'm so sorry. Maybe there's been enough healing time that you two can talk it out." Pausing, she gazed into his eyes, hoping and praying he'd take her advice to heart.

Ryan merely shrugged and backed away. "Yeah,

well, don't hold your breath. I just didn't want to disappear without telling you. And I wanted to make sure you weren't mad at me."

"I'm not mad." Her smile broadened and she rolled her eyes to indicate her parents lingering in the distance. "There may be a certain mayor who's not pleased with either of us, but I'm fine. I held my ground."

The lighthearted comment seemed to have the desired effect, because Ryan finally smiled back at her. "I wish I'd been there to hear you standing up to him."

"No, you don't," Julie said quickly. "Believe me, it wasn't pretty."

"It would have had to be pretty if you were there."

Her cheeks warmed. "Thanks. So take care, okay?"

"I will. Look for me sometime before next weekend."

"Is that a promise? Because it's going to be the best three days of all. We have lots of previous champions entered— besides you, I mean."

"Yeah, I know. It's going to be a pleasure outriding all of them."

Julie beamed. "I see your humility is as strong as ever."

"I'll mostly be showing off for my favorite sheep rancher."

"So how many of us do you know?" Julie drawled.

"Only one, Lambchop," he replied, finally breaking into a full grin. "That's way more than enough."

The urge to take off for Bozeman that very night was so strong Ryan had to talk himself out of leaving immediately.

Common sense prevailed, and he waited until the following morning. He'd thought about phoning first to make sure his mother was home, then decided it would be easier on both of them if he showed up unannounced.

By the time he completed the drive, however, he was as emotionally worn out as if he'd just ridden ten broncs in a row.

The old neighborhood seemed the same, as shabby and depressing as ever. Young men who should have been at work on a Monday morning lolled along the sidewalk and gathered at the occasional bus-stop bench. It didn't matter how they dressed or the color of their skin. They were as much alike as if they were wearing a sloppy uniform.

He slowed, then stopped in front of the brownstone his mother had moved into shortly after he'd hit the road for keeps. Her excuse had been that she had no more need for a bigger place. Ryan wasn't fooled. She was clearly having as much trouble getting past Kirk's absence in their former home as he had.

An older, gray-haired woman was sweeping the steps. She smiled at him. "Morning. Who you lookin' for, cowboy?"

"Carla Travers. She's my mother."

As he started past the woman, she touched his arm. "You're Ryan?"

"Yes, ma'am."

"Praise the Lord!" There were unshed tears in her eyes. "I been prayin' you'd come home."

"I was competing in Jasper Gulch. It was close," he alibied. "I'm not staying long."

"Doesn't matter." Cupping a hand around her mouth, she lowered her voice. "Your mama's been powerful lonesome, 'specially since a close friend of hers passed on. I tried to help her, but she keeps blamin' herself for everything."

Ryan backed off, scowling. "I don't understand."

"You will. You just talk to her for a little while and she's bound to open up to you like she has to me, you bein' her kin and all. If she clams up, you stop at my place before you go. I'm in number two, bottom floor, same as Carla."

"Okay." He was deep in thought and frowning when he knocked on his mother's apartment door. No one responded. He knocked again, harder.

"All right, all right, keep your shirt on. I'm comin'."

He was taking his hat off when the door swung open and he was faced with a person he hardly recognized. Instead of the orangey-dyed hair he remembered, this woman was totally gray. Her eyes were reddened and puffy.

If she hadn't been crying before, she certainly was now. Her jaw sagged. Her eyes widened, then seemed to sparkle as she reached for him.

Touched beyond imagining, Ryan opened his arms and she promptly hugged the breath out of him. Could he have caused this? Wasn't it bad enough that he'd been responsible for his brother's death without inadvertently hurting his mother, too?

With an arm around her shoulders, he ushered her into the apartment and kicked the door shut with his boot. What could he say? How could he hope to make this up to her?

"I'm sorry I haven't been by more often," he began. "It was selfish of me. I am so, so sorry."

Carla grabbed a handful of tissues and blew her nose before answering. "Nonsense. This is my fault, not yours. I should get out more, make new friends. It's just been so hard lately. I did find a nice church, though. Those folks have been won-derful to me."

"Church? You go to church?"

"Of course I do." She plopped herself down on the sagging sofa.

He joined her. "But…you never used to."

"I hardly had time to sleep when you were a boy, let alone go anywhere," she explained. "I was working two jobs to make ends meet."

"I knew that, I guess, just never thought of it that way. Kirk and I were alone so much it seemed unfair."

"That it was," she said, blotting the last of her happy tears. "Can I get you a soda? Coffee? Tea?"

"I'd rather you relaxed and sat here with me."

"My pleasure. You're looking wonderful, Ryan. The rodeo agrees with you. I was kind of afraid for you at first. I've been keeping up with your scores on the internet and I see you're doing very well."

"Yes. I am. You've been getting my checks, too, haven't you?"

"Sure have. As nice as that is, I'd trade 'em all for this visit. How long can you stay?"

"I'm competing in Jasper Gulch next weekend." Although he'd had no intention of hanging around longer than a day or so, if that, his conscience insisted he linger, at least until he found out more about his mother's problems.

"I saw you were ahead. They scrap those totals for the finals, though, don't they?"

"Yes. We all start again on an equal footing next Friday night."

"Well, never you mind. You'll do fine. You were right about making rodeo a career. Most men, like your daddy, can only dream about living the life you do. I'm proud you're such a success."

"Dad was a rodeo rider? You never told me that before."

"Because I didn't want it to influence you," Carla said. "You needed to find your own way, not try to follow in the footsteps of a man like him. I suspect he thought he could settle down and be a good husband and father, but it just wasn't in him."

"Where is he now?"

She shrugged. "Don't know. Don't really care. After he left, I poured all my love into you two boys until…"

Ryan was on the edge of losing control of his emotions. Nevertheless, he plunged ahead. "I'm so sorry. I should have told you Kirk was drinking and running around with a bad crowd. He made me promise I'd keep his secret, so I did. If I'd had any idea he was risking his life, I'd have told you anyway."

"It's not your fault, it's mine." She blotted a stray tear and tried to smile. "I should have kept better track of you boys. It was Kirk's job to look after you, not the other way around, and it was my job to take care of you both. I failed."

"But I thought…"

"What?" Sniffling, she gazed fondly at her youngest son.

"I thought you blamed me. I know I blamed myself."

"For your older brother's mistakes? Don't be silly, Ryan. Kirk was the one who made the choice to drink and drive."

"In that case, his death can't be your fault, either," he countered, watching to see if she agreed. "He and I had the same upbringing, and I don't drink, so how can his poor choices be because of anything you did or didn't do?"

Carla heaved a noisy sigh, then another, before she said, "You may be right. It sure felt like failure, though. You were so withdrawn afterward I figured you blamed me, too. When you went on the road full-time, I had terrible struggles coming to terms with it. At least at first."

"You looked pretty upset when I got here," Ryan told her. "What's wrong? Why are you so sad? Is it because I've been neglecting you?"

Her light laugh was a surprise to him.

"Mercy, no. A dear friend of mine passed away recently and I was sitting here feeling sorry for myself when you knocked on my door." She began to smile wistfully. "Maybe the good Lord sent you just when I most needed a lift. Who knows?"

Ryan leaned back and studied her. "I know somebody who would sure like to think I'm that close to God."

"Really? Who?"

When he said, "Her name is Julie," his mother grabbed his hand and held tight. The grin on her face was so wide and made her look so much like her old self again, he could hardly wait to tell her the whole story.

Chapter Sixteen

The four days between the time Ryan bid Julie goodbye at the church and the next rodeo were by far the longest in all of her twenty-four years.

She'd taken out her cell phone and stared at it repeatedly, knowing she could touch base with Ryan anytime with the push of a button, yet reluctant to disturb him.

"Besides, what would I say?" she muttered, disgusted at feeling unsettled. She'd known the handsome cowboy for less than a month, so why was he constantly on her mind and in her dreams?

Because we connected almost instantly, she answered without doubt. "I knew the minute I laid eyes on him that he was the one."

Julie jumped when her sister spoke. "Good for you."

She wheeled. "Whoa! I didn't hear you come in."

Faith merely smiled sweetly. "Probably because

you were off in la-la land with a certain rodeo rider I could mention."

"I do have it bad, don't I?"

"Looks like it to me." Faith patted her younger sister's shoulder. "Hang in there. We know he'll be back before tonight's performance."

"He said he would. It's just been so long without hearing a peep out of him that I'm worried he's changed his mind."

"About romance, maybe," Faith said wisely. "About winning the Jasper Gulch rodeo, no way. That guy is so focused it's a wonder he made any time for you."

"I suppose you're right. I sure have missed seeing him."

"You said he went to visit his mother, right?"

Julie nodded. "Uh-huh. She lives in Bozeman."

"So that's not far." She gave Julie's shoulder another soothing pat. "Simmer down, kid, or he'll think you're desperate."

Rolling her eyes and blushing, Julie replied, "I'm afraid I am."

Faith chuckled. "Well, see that you hide it unless you want to scare him off. Men don't seem to fall in love as easily as women do." She laughed again. "Except maybe poor Wilbur. He acts ready to propose to the first girl who smiles at him."

"I know. I really hope he finds a nice wife and the happiness he deserves. I'm sure there must be a woman out there somewhere who'll fit him."

"I did hear he's been looking on the internet," Faith told her. "The pickings in Jasper Gulch are pretty slim."

"For us, too," Julie reminded her. "Until I met Ryan, I was positive I'd never find a man who appealed to me."

"You're sure he's the right one?"

Julie felt her cheeks burning. She nodded. "I'm sure. Now all I have to do is convince Ryan. God must be sick of hearing me pray about it so often."

"Uh-uh. Prayer is fine as long as you're asking the right thing for the right reasons," Faith reminded her.

"I know. It started with my wish that Ryan would find peace and healing after he told me about his brother's accidental death. Then I started including a renewal of his faith. If—when—all that happens, I figure he and I will have a chance together."

"If not?"

Sobering, Julie shrugged. "If not, then I guess I'll have to rethink everything."

"Or wait on the Lord."

"Yeah. I sure wish I had more patience."

"Oh, no. Don't pray for that, whatever you do,

unless you're ready to be tested even more to improve it the hard way."

"I know. That's similar to what Pastor Ethan said when I talked to him recently. When Ryan asked me why I bothered praying since I claimed to trust God, I didn't know how to answer him about that, either."

"You could have said there's a lot we have to accept by faith without totally understanding it. Until he comes to the Lord and turns over control of his life, he won't have a clue. After that, it may not get much clearer for a while, but I can guarantee he'll feel better about everything."

"I know." Julie sighed as she met her sister's matching blue gaze. "It would probably be a lot easier for nonbelievers if Christians didn't make so many mistakes."

"I wonder," Faith replied. "If we were too perfect, it might seem like an unattainable goal to an outsider."

That irrefutable logic made Julie smile. "You're right. And considering the way I seem to be floundering, I can promise you I will not handle my emotions with anything near perfection. I'll be doing well to behave even halfway normally when Ryan comes back and I see him again."

Joining in the fun, Faith said, "Honey, I hate to be the one to break it to you. As far as I'm concerned, you're not *that* normal on your best days!"

* * *

Before Ryan left Bozeman, he was regaled by many of his mother's friends, most of whom also attended her church. That was how he learned more about the elderly gentleman Carla was currently mourning. She and the man had come to rely heavily on each other, so when he had died suddenly, his absence had left her despondent.

One element about the way she was dealing with that loss puzzled Ryan enough that he decided to ask, waiting until he was ready to head back to Jasper Gulch before broaching the tender subject. His mother was hugging him goodbye when he said, "There's something that confuses me."

She looked up. "About your brother?"

Ryan shook his head and pressed his lips into a thin line. "No. I understand about that now. As long as you and I don't blame ourselves, or each other, for what happened to Kirk, we'll both be fine."

"I agree. So what's troubling you?"

"The way you're coping, I guess. I know you gave up on Dad long ago, but you had something special going with the friend who died recently. Right?"

"Yes. I miss him every minute of every day."

"Then how can you smile so easily around your friends and seem to enjoy life the way you do? How did you get past your grief?"

Carla's smile was wistful and gentle. She laid her hand on her son's arm and he felt an instant connection.

"I'm not done grieving, honey. I don't think I ever will be. Sadness comes and goes. Some days are better than others. I just have to keep living, for his sake as well as my own, and remind myself that we'll meet again someday in heaven."

"How can you possibly know that?"

"Because we shared our beliefs. We both had faith in God and Jesus Christ." Her smile trembled; her eyes shone. "There are folks who claim to have all the answers. I'm not one of them. All I know is that the Lord has given me peace and is with me constantly. After all, He sent you here and brought us back together at just the right time, even though you had no idea how much I needed to reconnect." She embraced him once more. "I love you, son. So does God."

"I love you, too, Mom. If you change your mind and decide to come to Jasper Gulch for the finals, give me a call and I'll meet you. I programmed my cell number into your phone."

"I'd rather watch it on TV so I can get an instant replay," she said with a grin. "Just take care of yourself. And tell that Julie girl your mama says hello."

His mother's parting words echoed in Ryan's heart and mind as he followed the main highway back to Jasper Gulch. Learning that she, too, was a Bible-believing Christian had really shaken him. Religion was supposed to be complicated, wasn't it? So how could it be as simple as she'd insisted?

Of course, he was glad she'd found peace. He'd never wish otherwise. He simply could not accept the concept that a person's faith was a choice they made. It seemed to him that God was too far away to even notice, let alone care what happened to anybody here on Earth, so why was he having such a hard time letting go of the notion that he might actually be wrong about that?

"Beats me," Ryan muttered.

With his mind on other things, he almost failed to see a semitruck ahead of him start to swerve. Pieces of steel-belted tire were flinging into the air at high speed. A blowout!

Ryan instinctively ducked. His hands gripped the wheel. Every muscle in his body clenched. He braced for impact. At these speeds he was going to be fortunate if he got out alive, let alone made it back to compete in the rodeo that evening.

All around him brakes and sliding tires squealed. Cars and trucks swerved, careened off the center divider and slammed into each other, making a horrendous racket.

Ryan's next moments seemed to pass in slow motion. He steered left and right by impulse rather than skill, coming out on the far side of the accident without a scratch on himself or his truck.

Awed and in shock, he eased his vehicle over to the shoulder of the highway where it would be out of the way and jogged back to see if he could help those who might have been injured.

"How did I get through this?" he muttered, staring at the carnage and seeing no space to account for his escape.

In the back of his mind, something told him he already knew how, yet he continued to resist accepting the concept of divine intervention. That was what Julie—and Carla—would be insisting if either of them was here.

Going from car to wrecked car, Ryan paused long enough to make sure nobody was trapped before he moved on. Someone with a flare was already directing oncoming traffic and he could hear sirens in the distance. Help was close!

"Thank God," he whispered, realizing belatedly that he had just said a real prayer. After that, it became easier.

"Father, thank You for bringing me through this," he said quietly. "And help these others to make it, too. I know I haven't been in church much for a while, but my mother believes You never gave up on me and I'd like to believe it, too."

His path led him to a collapsed sedan with its windows smashed. Inside, he could see a child in a safety seat. She was whimpering but apparently unhurt. The car's driver was trapped in front by the folded steel but also conscious and fairly alert.

"My little girl!" the woman gasped. "Is she all right?"

"Yes, ma'am. She looks fine."

"Get her out. Please!"

"The firefighters are almost here," Ryan told her. "It's better if you don't try to move, either. Let them do their jobs, okay?" He waved his arms to attract first responders' attention to the car. "Here they come. You'll be free in no time."

"Don't leave us!"

"I won't. I promise. Just let me take a closer look in the back. Were there only two of you?"

"Yes. Yes…I…"

Ryan leaned through the shattered rear window to approach the frightened, towheaded child. "It's going to be okay, honey. You and your mama will be out of this mess in no time."

The tear-streaked face she lifted to look at him was more than hopeful. It was relieved and almost joyful. Ryan smiled at her.

"Promise?" she asked.

"I promise."

"Are you Jesus?" the little girl asked innocently.

"Nope, just one of His helpers," Ryan replied without hesitation.

In his heart he knew he had spoken the absolute truth. It wasn't merely that he was thankful for having survived. It was more. Much more. Somehow, in the midst of all this turmoil, he had taken the final step of acceptance. He was home and forgiven, just like the prodigal son.

Julie paced the rodeo grounds, anxious about Ryan and mad at herself for trusting him in the first place. He'd given his word. He was supposed to be there. So why wasn't he?

She spotted a red truck enter the fairgrounds, a cloud of reddish dust billowing behind it. Could that be him? Had he returned after all?

In spite of her prior determination to act nonchalant and try to make him believe she wasn't crazy about him, she broke into a wide grin and jogged to where he was parking.

"You cut that really close," she shouted. "Grab your gear. I hear the announcer. Bareback is about to start."

Ryan had jumped down and was pulling his rigging out of the back of the truck. "I know. I was afraid I wouldn't make it."

She could tell by his appearance that something was wrong. "What happened? Is your mother all right?"

"She's fine. There was a bad accident on the highway. I stopped to help out."

"You're okay?"

"Yes. Just tired." He swung his saddle over one shoulder and hoisted a crammed duffel bag. "I'm thankful nobody was killed."

"So am I." She gestured toward the arena. "You'd better run. Give me your keys and I'll lock up for you."

There was no hesitation on Ryan's part, further convincing her that he trusted her. Of course he did. They were friends, right? And *more* than that, if anybody wanted her opinion.

She made sure the truck's windows were rolled up and the doors locked, including the one on the matching camper shell, before she pocketed Ryan's keys and started for the grandstand. Without checking the evening's schedule, she couldn't be certain of the lineup. As long as Ryan reported before the final ride in his division, he should be allowed to compete even if he missed the first call-up.

When Julie reached the stands, she found Faith and Hannah waiting for her at the fence closest to the chutes.

Faith waved an arm. "Over here. Did he make it?"

Julie nodded, knowing her ear-splitting grin was all the answer anyone would need.

"Great! You want to stand here or look for higher seats so we can see better?"

"Higher, I guess," Julie said. Now that she'd

seen Ryan again, there was absolutely no doubt in her mind that she wanted to spend the rest of her life with him. To her regret, she was also thinking about how she could hang on to her flock and still follow him from rodeo to rodeo. The logistics of it would be difficult, but she'd manage, even if she had to hire daily help and turn over the basic management of the operation to one of her brothers.

They wouldn't like looking after sheep, but they'd do it for her. The Shaws always took care of one another no matter what.

"Dad is going to go ballistic," she muttered, leading the way up the grandstand tiers. Jackson was already acting more upset every day that the time capsule remained unaccounted for. Add to that all his concerns about upcoming centennial events and she could see why he'd not want to deal with her attraction to any man who wasn't from Jasper Gulch.

With a sigh, Julie edged into a narrow row and made room for her sister and best friend.

"So tell us." Hannah leaned to peer past Faith. "How did he react when you threw your arms around his neck and told him you were madly in love with him?"

Julie rolled her eyes. "Oh, yeah. Like that's going to happen."

"Why not? He did kiss you. Everybody who was there said it was very romantic."

"He was teasing," Julie argued. "That's hardly the same as sweeping me off my feet."

"It would work for me," Faith chimed in. "I haven't had a great kiss since…" She waved her hands in front of her face. "Never mind."

All three young women were laughing. The celebratory atmosphere at the rodeo contributed to their elation, of course, but Julie had an even better reason to be joyful. Ryan was back. He would win. He would keep competing and therefore would stay for the next three days at least.

Was that long enough for her to gather the courage, change her mind and explain how she felt about him? Would he be in the mood to listen to the plans she'd formed and agree to give their budding relationship a fair chance to bloom?

Naturally she would have preferred that they have a slow, sensible courtship instead of a rushed one. But that was not how this situation was turning out and, if she truly trusted God for her future, it was wrong to question His methods—or His results.

She momentarily closed her eyes and said a quick prayer for Ryan. And for herself. If the Lord's decision did not include Ryan's expression of mutual love and a promise of commitment, she didn't know how she'd react. It was going to be a struggle for her to accept less with grace and proper gratitude.

Chapter Seventeen

Scoring started from zero when the rodeo resumed for the third weekend. Ryan placed second in bareback on his first ride, missing the win by only half a point and making up the difference in the second round. There were so many rodeo champions and celebrities behind the chutes, TV and radio sportscasters kept shoving microphones in the face of any cowboy who didn't dodge them.

He agreed to give a short interview between bareback and saddle-bronc riding, allowing himself to be accosted only so he could also say hello to Carla and her friends in Bozeman. He'd meant to phone her between events, but in his hurry to get to the arena he'd left his phone in his truck and didn't have her number memorized. It had occurred to him to send Julie back to the truck for his cell since she already had the keys, but he didn't see her.

Things were moving along so fast he had little time to worry and none to waste searching the stands for her. He did scan the box where dignitaries and TV personalities sat. A few of the Shaws were in attendance, including the mayor. Julie had apparently chosen to sit elsewhere.

He didn't spot her again until after his second saddle-bronc ride. The saddle was slung over his shoulder and he was standing there, wondering how he was going to get into his locked truck to get his bull rope, when she appeared.

The keys jingled as she held them up. "Looking for these?"

"Yes. I wondered where you'd gone."

"I was in the stands with Faith and Hannah. You made some really great rides."

"Thanks. It's still close for the overall championship. There's a lot of talent here this weekend."

"We won't really know until Sunday night, will we?"

"Not unless one of us runs away with the points total before then. The way things are shaping up, it looks as if it may be decided on the final rides."

"Makes it more exciting for the fans."

Ryan had to agree. "For us riders, too, although I can't say I'd mind having a bigger lead than anybody else by then. That last bull is always the most nerve-racking, not counting the bonus-money ride for whoever wins."

He noticed her beginning to frown. "What's wrong?"

"I kind of thought you might bring your mom back with you. I'd like to meet her."

"I did invite her. She said she likes to watch the action on television so she gets instant replays."

"I can understand that. All I did was blink and I missed one of your get-offs."

"At least I landed on my feet every time tonight."

"That is a plus."

She was smiling again and her blue eyes were twinkling. Oh, how he was going to miss her when he hit the road again. He loved—liked—so much about her, from her pretty auburn hair to the tips of her dusty cowboy boots.

It was the kindness, the tenderness, in her expression that touched him the most, he realized. He'd thought the main attraction was her quick wit and loveliness, but there was much more to Julie than that. Now that he'd returned and was with her again, he could feel a difference that was almost palpable. Exactly what that change might be and how it had come about was a puzzle that had no easy solution.

Keep your mind on your riding or you'll be sorry, he warned himself. There was a right time and a wrong time to make his position clear to Julie. In the middle of an important competition was definitely the wrong time to be dealing with volatile emotions, hers or his own.

He would eventually speak his mind, Ryan vowed. And when he did, he'd try to let her down easy. He'd be diplomatic, speak sensibly and reason with her. She'd be fine in the long run. He knew she would be.

And, without a doubt, he also knew that he would *not* be okay. Not even close. He simply refused to walk in his father's footsteps and fool himself into believing he could settle down in one place and find happiness. The more he cared for Julie, the more she reminded him of Carla and the struggles she'd faced because she'd foolishly fallen in love with a roving cowhand.

The most loving thing Ryan could do for Julie was bid her a fond goodbye and drop out of her life, so that was what he'd do. For her sake. Even if it broke his heart.

Julie wasted little time checking on the way her father chose to spend the evening. Why would she when Ryan was front and center? He finished his last bull ride beautifully, earning ninety points and outdoing every other rider.

To her chagrin, that score drew hordes of reporters and TV cameras as well, keeping her at bay until the furor died down.

He loved competing. She could see it in his expression, in his proud posture and the competent way he spoke to the interviewers. There was no way she could take this from him unless he voluntarily offered to change his schedules and compete nearer to her, at least long enough for their romance to develop.

Julie sobered. If she spoke up and confessed her love, he might think she was trying to manipulate him into quitting. Although that would simplify her life, she knew it would be wrong to even hint at. The decision to continue to see her had to come from him—before she offered to follow him when he traveled—or she would never be certain of his true feelings.

Coercion was wrong. She knew that. It was just that keeping her love for him to herself was terribly difficult.

By the time Ryan finally broke away and rejoined her, he was obviously exhausted. She looped her arm through his. "Tired?"

"That's an understatement."

"Then you probably should go get some rest."

"You trying to get rid of me?"

Julie could tell he was slightly put off in spite of his lighthearted facade. "Not at all. I thought maybe we could meet at Great Gulch Grub tomorrow for a late breakfast. That will give me time to do my chores early."

"I could bring breakfast to your place again," he offered.

"I know. And I appreciate the offer, it's just that..."

"Your father won't appreciate it."

"There is that. And I think we'd be more comfortable if we didn't have to worry about anybody dropping by the house and interrupting. If we can't find a quiet booth in a corner, we can always go outside to talk and sit in one of our trucks."

"You're starting to sound really serious. Is something wrong that you haven't told me?"

"No, no. Everything's good. I just want some peace and quiet so you can tell me all about your visit with your mother. Was she glad to see you?"

"Oh, yeah. You probably noticed that I extended my stay and hung around Bozeman for a few extra days."

"I had wondered what became of you."

"Why didn't you call me if you were worried?"

Julie rolled her eyes. "Why didn't you call *me* if you were worried that I was worried?"

"Because I wasn't worried," Ryan replied with a satisfied-looking grin. "Did you expect me to be?"

"Of course not."

"Well, then, we're all right. Right?"

"Right." She tried to think of another play on words and failed, so she simply stayed beside him until they reached his red pickup.

Ryan stowed the last of his gear in the back. "So what time?"

"Huh?"

He chuckled, his eyes sparkling in the twilight. "Saturday-morning breakfast. It was your idea, remember? What time shall we meet?"

"Oh. Let's say eight, if that's not too late for you."

"That'll be fine."

As soon as he'd slammed the door to the camper shell, he stepped back and shoved his hands into his pockets, clearly demonstrating no desire to hug or kiss her goodbye, much to Julie's chagrin.

She assumed a casual pose in self-defense. "Okay, then. We're all set. Have a good night."

"You, too."

It was all she could do to stand still instead of throwing herself into his arms. If Ryan had not turned away and circled to the driver's side of his truck at that moment, she feared she might have embarrassed them both.

The engine hummed. He shifted. Started to drive away.

Julie felt rooted to the spot. Unsure. Disappointed. And wondering if she had been misreading him all along.

"Well, what if I was?" she grumbled. "At least my pride is intact."

A lot of good her pride would do her if Ryan kept to his previous plans and hit the road after the last night of the rodeo. Surely he must know how she felt about him. After all, they had shared that amazing kiss.

The mere thought of it gave her the shivers. If that man was even a tenth as impressed as she was, there was no way he'd ride off into the sunset like the hero in an old Western movie.

She had to smile at that notion. There was a lot about Ryan that reminded her of the old-fashioned morals and habits she'd grown up with. He was a real gentleman, a person she was proud to call a friend and not a bit shy to be seen with. The way he'd stepped right into her daily routine and helped with the sheep had been amazing. Yes, he could be a tease, but there was no rancor in his wit. On the contrary, he made her feel accepted. Loved.

Loved? Not exactly. He may have kissed her in public, but after that she'd gotten the impression he was avoiding her as much as possible.

It probably didn't help that her father had made him feel about as welcome as a skunk at a church picnic, she reasoned, chagrined. Well, there wasn't anything she could do about that except pray that her family mellowed, particularly the male contingent. Adam had seemed okay with her interest in Ryan, but Cord and Austin were more ambivalent. And, of course, there was always Dad. Jackson Shaw had a well-practiced icy stare that could freeze a lake in July.

Which was almost over, Julie realized, counting the remaining days. The month had raced by since she'd first noticed Ryan at the parade. That encounter sometimes seemed a lifetime away. Other times it felt as if it had happened yesterday. She knew a lot about him. She also had to admit that there must be a million important details she had yet to discover.

The question was not what those facts might be. It was whether Ryan was going to give her a chance to learn them.

Faith was waiting by Julie's truck when she returned to it. "So how did it go? I saw you two walk off together."

"He was tired. He went home."

"Well, that's certainly disappointing. Did he say anything special?"

"Like what?"

Her sister rolled her eyes. "Oh, I don't know. Maybe that he'd missed you or was crazy about you."

Making a face, Julie shook her head. "Nope. Nothing like that. Unfortunately."

"Did you give him a chance? I mean, you

weren't hanging out behind the chutes the way you used to."

"Only because I didn't want to be a distraction. This last weekend is very important to all the riders and ropers."

"Yeah, yeah, I get it. I just don't want to see you let him leave Jasper Gulch without telling him how you feel."

"I don't know that myself."

"Yes, you do. Admit it. You're in love with him."

"What if I am? I don't intend to commit to him before I'm certain he's ready. I've seen a lot of women throw themselves at rodeo cowboys. I don't want him to think I'm like them."

"He sure won't as long as you keep beating around the bush, little sister. Would it hurt you to flirt just a little? Huh?"

"I don't know how to turn my feelings on and off like a faucet," Julie replied. "And I wouldn't want to try, even if I thought I was good at it. The best times Ryan and I had were when we kicked back, enjoying each other's company. Now that I care so much, it's like I'm brain-dead and tongue-tied."

"Now, *there's* an interesting picture. I don't suppose you want me to take him aside and wise him up?"

"No!" Julie realized belatedly that she was shouting and muted the rest of her response. "No, no, no. I've made up my mind to wait until Ryan speaks up first. If I tell him I love him, that will put him in an impossibly difficult position unless he feels the same about me."

"Looks to me like he does."

"I'm not so sure." She was slowly shaking her head as she folded her arms across her chest. "There were times I thought so, but since he came back from seeing his mother he's acted distant."

"*That* you could ask him about, couldn't you?"

"Yes. And I will. Tomorrow morning we're meeting for breakfast and I'm going to bring it up then."

Faith reached out and hugged her sister, then bid her good-night. "Okay. Be good. I'll talk to you after you and the love of your life have had a chance to chat."

"He is, you know," Julie said wistfully.

"I really hope so," her sister said in parting. "For your sake."

"Me, too," Julie murmured.

Being a weekend morning and given all the tourists in town, Ryan wondered if they were going to get a table in the café before lunchtime. He'd arrived early and grabbed a back booth the moment one was available, hoping that Julie would figure out where he was and venture inside instead of waiting for him on the sidewalk.

When he saw her come through the door and look around the room, he rose and waved.

Watching her already pretty face brighten the moment she spied him made his own heart pound. He knew his grin was so wide it must look silly, but he couldn't help himself. He stood, waiting, and saw Julie pause to speak to a studious-looking young woman. To his chagrin, they approached the booth together.

"This is Robin Frazier," Julie told Ryan. "The researcher I told you about."

He shook her hand, hoping she didn't intend to join them. "My pleasure."

"How's your work going?" Julie asked her.

"Fair. I'm still looking for more personal information about the town's founding. Your family wouldn't happen to have an album I could look at, would they?"

"Not one that goes back that far," Julie replied.

"How about family folklore? Anything that pertains to the old-time families? You must have heard stories growing up."

"I can't say I remember anything unusual," Julie said. Ryan noticed that she was beginning to frown and hoped the other woman would back off soon.

With a sigh, Robin nodded. "Well, be sure to keep me in mind if you think of any." She looked to Ryan, nodded and said, "Pleased to meet you," before taking her leave.

As soon as Julie was seated, he asked, "Is that woman always so persistent about her work?"

"I hadn't really noticed it before. She did seem overly nosy, didn't she?"

"Sure did. Makes me wonder what she's up to."

"Probably just dedicated."

"If you say so." Ryan poured her a cup of hot coffee from the carafe on the table.

"Thanks. You think of everything."

"I have to confess. The pot was Mert's idea. She said it would save her steps, but I think she was being nice and hated to admit it."

"Probably. She and Rusty really sound like a couple of curmudgeons when they tease each other, but you've gotta love 'em."

"Speaking of the old guy, I haven't seen him lately. Is he okay?"

"Far as I know. I think patrolling the parking lots at the fairgrounds is harder on him than he likes to admit. He's been putting in long hours. I imagine he's sleeping late when he can."

"I slept in, too," Ryan said as he stirred cream into his coffee and offered the container to Julie. "Sorry you had to get up so early to do chores. You should have let me come and help you again."

"Not this week. It's too important. You need to save your energy for riding."

"You're probably right. That's another reason my mom decided to stay in Bozeman. She said I needed to keep my focus on the rodeo."

"She's right. You do. But nothing says we can't meet for meals now and then. Do you have any special regimen you stick to before a rodeo?"

"Other than not pigging out, no," Ryan told her. "Some of the guys think there are special foods that help or they have superstitions they follow. Not me. I work out in a gym whenever I can, but I'm not obsessive about it. Yet. As I get older I imagine I'll have to train harder to stay up with the young guns."

"How long do you expect to keep riding?"

Ryan shrugged. "Who knows? Some guys stay into their thirties and beyond. If I can squeeze out another ten years or so, I'll consider myself blessed. After that wreck I was almost caught in on my way back from Bozeman, I'm positive God is looking after me."

"You are?"

"Uh-huh." Pensive, he folded his hands atop the table and laced his fingers together. "I'm still not exactly sure what all happened, but I did come out of it reconnected to God. There's no doubt in my mind."

"That's wonderful!"

"I thought you'd be pleased. My mother was

when I phoned her last night, too. It seems you were both praying for me."

"And we won't stop now," Julie assured him. "How did she take it when you talked about your brother? You did, didn't you?"

Ryan nodded sagely and sobered. "Yes. It turns out we were each blaming ourselves instead of holding Kirk responsible for his own actions. I had no idea she was feeling guilty, too."

"Then you can put it behind you?"

"In a manner of speaking. Mom just lost a really good friend. The way she explained it, she'll always miss him, she'll just go on with her life because he'd want her to."

"So does God," Julie added.

"I agree. So now that we've solved the problems of the world around us, what would you like for breakfast?"

He could tell by her expression that she wanted to probe deeper into his psyche, but Ryan was reluctant. The more she knew about his past, the more likely she'd be to feel sorry for him, and that was the last thing he wanted.

Julie was a wonderful girl—woman—and her father was right. She deserved a man who had roots, who would support her efforts on the ranch and love her enough to settle down. To stay. No matter how much he thought he could be that man right now, no matter how strongly he wished to be, deep down he feared he might be too much like his absentee father. After all, they both had trouble staying put for very long.

Carla had evidently sensed that part of his personality and had wisely withheld some information about his dad until a few days ago. In retrospect, Ryan understood her reasoning; he simply didn't like being left in the dark to find his own way.

It wasn't surprising that his instincts had led him down the same path in spite of his mother's secrets. Like all men, he needed to be true to his inner drives in order to function properly.

What about falling for a small-town girl? Ryan asked himself. *How stupid was that?*

Plenty, he answered internally, but that didn't mean he had to hurt Julie in order to help himself cope. The only fair thing, the only right choice, was to leave town without letting on how he felt. She was a sensible person. She'd eventually get over him.

That thought was so painful he almost winced. If he hadn't caught her looking across the table at him with those beautiful blue eyes and her sweet smile, he might have gotten up and left the café then and there.

Chapter Eighteen

Saturday morphed into Sunday before Julie could decide where she had gone wrong or make sense of Ryan's actions. He had seemed ready to have a personal discussion with her in Great Gulch Grub, then had clammed up as if her father was standing right behind him, looking over his shoulder.

Try as she might, she could not figure out why Ryan had begun acting so vague. She had expected his return to his faith to be a blessing, not a roadblock to their relationship, yet she could think of nothing else he'd mentioned that might be so influential.

Unless she'd been right when she'd initially considered their meeting to be in God's plans for saving him, she reasoned. If so, perhaps she had played her part and was now finished. Talk about a depressing thought!

She was still thinking, mulling things over and

praying about her confusion after church. If the final day of the rodeo had not been so important to her, in many ways, she might have spent her afternoon and evening out among her flock where nobody cared what kind of mood she was in and no one asked leading questions.

Except for Cowboy Dan, she thought, giving his silky ears a gentle ruffle. The dog had obviously sensed her unrest because he was refusing to leave her side. Normally that wouldn't have been a problem, but since she was headed for the rodeo arena for the last time, she hesitated.

"I'm okay, boy," Julie said softly. "It's okay. You need to stay home and wait for me." She pointed to her porch. "Stay."

The intelligent Australian shepherd was having no part of that order. He scooted so close she could feel him actually leaning against her leg.

Julie sighed. Dan had always been an intuitive animal. And until today, she had paid heed to his signals. Given that his companionship was comforting, she decided to listen again and take him along.

"Okay, get in the truck. But you have to be on a leash," Julie warned, pulling one from behind the seat in the cab after he'd jumped aboard.

The dog's ensuing reaction made her chuckle. Poor Dan could be the poster boy for a hangdog look at the moment. His head was lowered, his ears laid back, his eyes peering up at her from behind lowered lashes as if he thought he was hiding from the dreaded tether that limited his freedom.

Those antics alone lifted her spirits. She'd already been nervous about Ryan's riding today, and her personal interest in the cowboy had intensified the existing emotional tension until she was every bit as wired as her sensitive dog. Taking Dan with her shouldn't be a problem. His calm, loving presence was just what she needed on a day like this.

The only thing she would have liked better was to have the rodeo over with so Ryan could act on whatever personal interest he had in her. He must be feeling something. He had to be. There was no way he'd missed picking up on her fondness—and more.

Julie slammed the truck door and turned the key. The rodeo finals had to be Ryan's hang-up, she concluded. He'd been concerned about her father's undue influence from the beginning. Therefore, it made perfect sense for him to behave nonchalantly toward her until the competition was completed and he'd won.

He will win, she told herself. In her opinion there were no riders who could match his skill and daring, no matter how many other champions happened to be in town.

The mottled-gray dog laid his chin on her right

knee and gazed up at her as if she was the most important person in his life.

The direct contrast between the dog's attitude and Ryan's amused her. She smiled. "Too bad you can't teach another favorite cowboy of mine to look at me that way all the time."

The dog wiggled his stump of a tail, clearly in agreement with anything Julie wanted, especially since she was treating him to a ride into town.

An old mentor of Ryan's had taught him that too much bravado in the chutes could be worse than being scared stiff. There was no danger of that today. He recognized his normal anxiety, the result of the surges of adrenaline that gave him his winning edge. This afternoon, however, he was sensing something else, a fear he could only interpret as an aura of impending doom.

It didn't help that his final round pitted him against a son of the infamous Panhandle Slim. This bull was enormous, an advantage for a taller rider like Ryan. It also had a hump; a broad, slanted back; and a reputation for coming after anybody who happened to be handy once he'd unseated his rider.

The bullfighters were already falling back as Ryan settled in place and nodded.

The gate swung open. Wranglers jumped clear of the snorting, rampaging animal.

It kept bucking, shifting Ryan's weight to the outside and beginning a tight spin at the same time.

Spectators were on their feet, cheering, hooting and whistling.

Ryan knew better than to look up and lose focus. His internal clock was ticking off the seconds.

Where was eight? The whistle should have blown. His hand was starting to come loose from the rigging. One more immense jump. Than another.

Finally! A horn blast. Ryan opened his gloved hand and let the bull's momentum throw him clear.

He landed on all fours, quickly jumping to his feet as the one-ton behemoth wheeled and made a beeline for him.

Several clowns crossed between rider and bull. The animal's attention was diverted for mere moments. That was enough to let Ryan scale the fence and stand on a rung near the top to salute his fans with a broad grin and fist pump.

He knew before the scores were tallied that he'd done it. He'd won. Everything. It was finally over.

Only it wasn't, was it? he reminded himself. There was still the awards presentation ceremony to get through before he would ride the bonus bull for an additional hundred thousand dollars. Even if he happened to fail to do that successfully, he'd come away from this extended rodeo with half a year's worth of winnings, thanks to all the generous sponsors and supporters. If he rode the auto industry–sponsored bonus bull, it didn't matter how high or low he scored as long as he stayed on for the full eight.

Congratulations from the grandstand and clusters of news reporters were just the beginning. Other riders smacked him on the back, gave him high fives and shook his hand as he made his way to the reviewing stand where the mayor and arena judges had gathered.

There were gold-and-silver belt buckles for some of the day leaders and monetary awards for ropers and steer wrestlers, so they were presented first. Ryan had been told to wait next to a hand-tooled, silver-embellished Western saddle and matching bridle, which were part of his winnings. Whether he kept them or eventually sold them wasn't important as long as he earned enough to adequately pad his savings account. In this case, the check for winning overall was going to be more than sufficient.

Jackson Shaw himself presented his award, a facsimile printed on a large sheet of poster board so it would be highly visible. He and Ryan shook hands and posed together while lights flashed and applause literally shook the platform.

"Thank you, sir," Ryan said.

Jackson was outwardly polite when he replied, "My pleasure," but his smile never affected his steely eyes.

Ryan reached for the microphone the mayor was holding. "I'd like to say a few words, if you don't mind."

If there had been no audience, Ryan figured Shaw would have denied him the right to speak. Since they were standing in front of most of the townspeople, as well as news cameras from all over Montana and beyond, the man conceded.

"Thanks." Ryan held up the awkwardly huge paper check and spoke into the microphone. "I want to thank all my fans and rodeo supporters for the chance to participate in this special competition."

He waited until the cheers died down before continuing. "I've made lots of friends here in Jasper Gulch and I want you all to know I'll never forget you."

As Ryan spoke, his eyes were raking the stands and checking both sides of the platform where he stood. He didn't see Julie, yet he knew she was there. She had to be. There was no way an avid rodeo fan like her would miss the finals, particularly his last rides.

It was the dog he spotted first. Cowboy Dan barked, drawing Ryan's attention to an area along a distant fence. Julie was perched atop it, watching intently, while her shepherd stood on the ground, sounding off every few seconds.

So this is it, he told himself. It was now or never. He set the cumbersome check replica aside and grasped the mic with both hands so nobody could tell if he was shaky.

"It's been great getting to meet you all and I've enjoyed our time together," Ryan began. *This is for you, Julie.* "But all good things must come to an end. I've been blessed to be here, and I promise if I'm ever in the neighborhood again, I'll try to make time to stop by and say hello."

There. He'd done it. Surely she'd understand and start looking for a local man who could make her happy. Somebody she could trust to be the kind of husband a woman like her deserved. Somebody stable and steady.

Most rodeo horses and bulls were from long lines of similar animals. They behaved the way they did because they had no choice. They had been born to buck. It was genetically inescapable. So was his heritage. That was why his mother had chosen to keep the truth from him and why ignorance of his birthright had made no difference in his career choices. He was just like his father had been, only more skilled and successful in his rodeo career.

Jackson reclaimed the mic. "There we are, ladies and gentlemen. Now, who wants to see our rough-stock champ ride for the bonus money?"

To Ryan's chagrin, he had forgotten all about having one more ride waiting.

Gloom descended over him when he looked back at the far fence. Julie was gone.

All she wanted to do was run and hide. If Dan had not insisted on sniffing every fence post and every blade of grass they passed, she'd have already been back in her truck and headed for home.

She gave the leash a sharp tug. "Come on, dog. Get a move on."

The busy canine didn't even bother to glance at her. Instead, he put his nose to the ground and kept pulling her along.

Julie sighed. What difference did it make where she went? Ryan was plainly leaving Jasper Gulch as soon as possible—and taking her heart with him. Chances of hearing him confess his love were slim to none, thanks to the finality of his farewell speech. She supposed it was just as well that he'd spelled it out for her, because she never would have believed it otherwise.

Meandering wherever the dog led her, she noticed a hush come over the arena. It took little time to realize why. Ryan was about to step aboard the bonus bull, a nasty, temperamental monster whose buck-off record rivaled that of his sire and grandsire.

She didn't want to watch. Didn't want to care. She simply had to look. Talking herself out of it was impossible.

Slammer was a grandson of the infamous bull Bodacious, the same yellowish-white color and with the same deadly habit of slinging his head. He had been ridden once out of thirty-seven outs, and that cowboy had vowed never to climb on him again.

Ryan knew all this. He also knew he owed it to the rodeo organizers and the folks in the stands to try to make the ride. Yes, the prize money was an incentive, but he would have tried this bounty bull if there had been nothing offered but the challenge. It was a matter of pride.

And stubbornness, he told himself as he wound the braided rope of the rigging around his glove and pounded his fingers tight with his opposite fist.

One thing was crystal clear. Every second he sat there gave Slammer more time to get wound up. The bull's neck muscles were already corded and he was blowing froth from his flared nostrils. This animal not only acted like a renegade, he looked the part, too.

Beige hair lay in curls between his horns. His

hump quivered as if he was trying to rid himself of a pesky barnyard fly.

"Yeah, like me," Ryan muttered, slipping his mouthpiece between his teeth and clamping down. It was now or never, and the anticlimactic feeling after winning the big check was more than a little unnerving. Still, if he wanted to please his corporate sponsors and keep making a name for himself in the sport, he'd have to do this. ASAP.

Ryan pushed his hat down tighter. Took a deep breath.

Then he clamped his heels to the bull's sides, turned out his toes, nodded his head and found himself hanging on to the rankest, most unpredictable tornado of a bucking bull he'd ever been on.

The closest his imagination could come to a description of his ride was the feeling a guy might have if he was strapped to the outside of a one-ton balloon and a giant was rapidly letting the air out of it.

Julie didn't scream. She was too shocked to make a sound. She'd never seen anything close to the way this bull was leaping and landing, only to launch himself again and turn a one-eighty while in the air!

Her gaze locked on Ryan. His free hand was still in the air and he seemed balanced, although how anybody could hope to have control over an unpredictable animal like Slammer was unthinkable. So far, the bull hadn't tried to fool Ryan and pull him forward for the kind of debilitating head butt his granddaddy was famous for, but the ride was barely half over. At the velocity he was bucking, he still had plenty of opportunity.

Julie grasped the top railing of the metal fence. She could barely breathe. Her head was spinning like Dan did when he got too excited.

"Oh, Ryan" was more of a prayer than a statement, and she followed it up with, "Please, please, God. Be with him and keep him safe. And alive."

Just then he began to slide to the outside, carried by centrifugal force. Julie gasped. Saw him make the adjustment to the inside of the spin.

Changing positions as if swapping ends in the air, Slammer reversed directions.

Ryan was unable to keep up. He started to slip, yet refused to open his hand and jump free.

Julie's screams were lost among those of the rest of the audience.

The bull's head whipped to the side where Ryan hung suspended by one hand and one spur.

Wild-eyed, Slammer was glaring at his rider from barely inches away.

He gave his big horns and head a toss, clipping Ryan's temple and sending his hat flying.

The sound of the impact was an audible *thunk*.

Bullfighters closed in. The whistle blew.

Ryan's hand was now wedged in the rigging. His spur came loose when he lost consciousness, leaving him hanging like a rag doll.

The bull kept lunging and spinning, trying to hook his senseless body with a horn to finish him off.

Julie finally screamed, "No!" The man she loved was going to die right in front of her eyes and she was helpless to stop it.

Without a thought for her own safety, she slid off the fence and dropped into the arena.

A blur shot past at the edge of her vision, heading straight for the injured cowboy and the wild bull.

"Dan! No!" She lunged for the trailing end of the leash and missed. This could not be happening.

Running forward, she bit back sobs. She was going to lose them both!

Ryan was only slightly aware he was in trouble. Years of training and well-honed survival instincts urged him to try to get his feet under him before he was trampled.

He heard Slammer bellow and the bullfighters start to curse. Then, suddenly, his hand was loose and he was being flung to the side.

Landing in loose dirt, he lay there, stunned, wondering where his adversary was and how soon he'd be freight trained, the slang term for being run down and smashed flat by horns and hooves.

A pickup horse passed close by at a gallop, its rider swinging a wide loop.

Ryan raised on one elbow to see if the rider was going to be able to lasso the bull and guide him out of the arena. Dust burned his eyes and his head throbbed as if he *had* been hit by a train.

Lights flashed. Men were yelling. A woman was screaming. A warm, wet tongue was licking his face. *Huh?*

Ryan fought to sit up. Several pairs of strong hands held him down. He tried to focus.

"Mmm," he groaned. "Must be dreaming."

"I wish we both were," Julie whispered, her lips only inches from his. "I thought I'd lost you before I had a chance to tell you."

Still groggy, Ryan was beginning to make sense of some of his current sensations. The only one that didn't fit was Julie on her knees in the dirt of the rodeo arena.

"Tell me what?" he mumbled.

"This. I don't care whether you like it or not or whether you stay or go. I'm crazy in love with you and I don't care who hears me say it."

"You don't mean that," Ryan mustered the strength to argue, although not as forcefully as he'd intended.

"I most certainly do." There were unshed tears

in Julie's eyes as she cupped his cheeks, leaned closer and kissed him. "Are you conscious enough to appreciate that?"

"I'm close," Ryan said. "But you must have gotten butted in the head, too, if you think I'm going to ruin your life by admitting I'm in love with you."

"I think you just did."

He waved off the medics as they continued to try to assess his physical state. "I'm injured. Out of my mind. I can't be held responsible for any idiotic babbling."

"Then I suppose you're going to claim my dog didn't just save your life."

"What?" He permitted the medics to help him sit up instead of transferring him to a backboard. If at all possible, he intended to leave the arena under his own steam. Right after he scolded Julie for coming anywhere near the inside when there was a bull present.

One of the nearby bullfighters spoke up, clearly disgusted. "Stupid mutt almost got us all killed when he latched on to that bull's nose with his teeth."

"Unbelievable," Ryan said. "He's supposed to be a heeler."

Julie rocked back, beaming and hugging her panting canine. "I guess Dan never read the sheepdog manual. When he saw you in trouble, he did what he had to do."

"Then I hope the mayor has a big checkbook," Ryan said as he was helped to his feet. "The stock contractor who owns Slammer is not going to be a happy camper."

She slid an arm around Ryan's waist while one of the medics supported him on the opposite side. They walked away, listening to a crescendo of applause and shouts from the crowd, with Dan trailing them.

"Well, I am," Julie told him. "Happy, I mean. I can't believe we were going to go our separate ways without telling each other how we felt."

"My dad deserted my mother," he said quietly. "I didn't know the details before my last visit, but I'd always suspected he ran out on her. That's the kind of dysfunctional family I come from."

"So? My father is a control freak who tends to abuse his power and try to run everything and everybody. Does that mean I'm like *him*?"

Ryan managed a smile as he drawled, "Well… you did jump into the arena to try to save me when you knew how crazy it was. I can understand your dog doing something that stupid, but I thought you had better sense."

"How do you know I didn't do it to rescue the dog?"

"Because it was me you said you were in love with."

The sound of her ensuing laughter did a lot to

heal his aches and pains. In the future, he knew it was going to be a sound he wanted to hear every single day for the rest of his life.

"Then I guess I'll have to marry you to keep you in line," he gibed, knowing that would set her off again.

"You sure will," she told him lovingly, tenderly. "You can go to rodeos all over the lower forty-eight and beyond if you want to, but it'll be with my ring on your finger."

"You are a bossy woman, Miss Peep."

She laughed lightly and kissed his dusty cheek. "Cowboy, when you're right, you're right."

Epilogue

Julie held up her hand to let Mert admire the diamond in her engagement ring, then turned back to Ryan. "You don't have to do this, you know."

He laughed. "What? Buy the ring or marry you?"

"Agree to be part of the Olde Tyme Wedding."

"I don't see why not." He bestowed a lopsided grin and arched an eyebrow. "Unless you've changed your mind and want to elope."

"I do and I don't," Julie said soberly. "I don't want to disappoint all my family and friends, but I don't want you to miss the finals in Vegas because of me, either."

"Not a problem. Really. I can catch it next fall as a spectator if I don't go to enough rodeos to accumulate the points to enter. This year I want to be here to supervise the details of our new house." His easy smile reflected pure contentment. "I'd always planned to buy a ranch of my own, I just never dreamed it would be so soon or that I'd end up raising sheep on it."

"Not exclusively," Julie replied. "You already have enough horses to supply an old-fashioned posse."

"Hey, I like to ride. It's a lot more fun than one of your dad's ATVs."

"Maybe." Over his shoulder she noticed rancher Jack McGuire joining them at the lunch counter. "That reminds me. Do you play baseball?" she asked Ryan.

His brow furrowed. "Not since I was a kid. Why?"

Julie leaned forward to peer past him and called, "Hey, Jack. I'd like you to meet Ryan Travers."

The men shook hands.

"My pleasure," McGuire said amiably.

"You the pro ballplayer Julie told me about?"

"I was going to turn pro," Jack said. "My plans were changed for me a long time ago."

Julie was pleased to see that Ryan's broad grin remained when he told Jack, "A guy's original ideas can change for the better without him even realizing it at first. I know mine have. I've just made a down payment on my own spread."

"Congratulations." McGuire leaned away and picked up his coffee mug.

Julie wasn't deterred. "You should think about helping with the baseball tournament next month, Jack. You have a lot to offer and it might be fun for a change. Team practice would at least get you off that ranch of yours and back into civilization once in a while."

Although the rancher merely shrugged, Julie was pleased to note that he had not turned her down flat. Dad and the other members of the centennial planning committee would be delighted to hear that.

As for her, she had other things on her mind. Slipping a hand around her fiancé's arm, she leaned closer to him and sighed. The newest citizen of Jasper Gulch was the dearest to her heart and took up nearly all her thoughts, waking and dreaming.

She could hardly wait for the big bash in October when she'd finally become Mrs. Ryan Travers. Good thing her wedding dress was going to be floor length like all the others. That way nobody would know she was shod in cowboy boots, and it could be a special surprise for her husband. It thrilled her to the core and gave her goose bumps to imagine his amazing laugh and the way his eyes would sparkle when he finally saw her feet.

The way Julie viewed their future, the boots

would be only one of the many surprises awaiting them, and she thanked God for bringing them together—from the bottom of her heart.

* * * * *

If you liked this BIG SKY CENTENNIAL
novel, watch for the next book,
HIS MONTANA SWEETHEART,
by Ruth Logan Herne,
available August 2014

And don't miss a single story in the
BIG SKY CENTENNIAL *miniseries:*

Book #1: HER MONTANA COWBOY
by Valerie Hansen

Book #2: HIS MONTANA SWEETHEART
by Ruth Logan Herne

Book #3: HER MONTANA TWINS
by Carolyne Aarsen

Book #4: HIS MONTANA BRIDE
by Brenda Minton

Book #5: HIS MONTANA HOMECOMING
by Jenna Mindel

Book #6: HER MONTANA CHRISTMAS
by Arlene James

Dear Reader,

As you may have noticed, I love small towns and rodeos. Cowboys don't make bad heroes, either! Maybe the hat and the boots contribute, but I think it's their character and quiet inner strength that makes many of them so special. Personally, I fell for the hat and six-guns. Never did get the horse!

In this story, Ryan believes his mistake is unforgivable then learns otherwise after suffering needlessly. If you take nothing else away from this book, I pray you will understand that in God's eyes, there is no sin that won't be forgiven if you confess it and turn to the Lord.

Blessings,

Valerie Hansen

Questions for Discussion

1. Are you interested in the sport of rodeo? Did you think of it in those terms before reading this book?

2. Does it seem natural to want to be on the road all the time or would you want a home base if you were a rider?

3. How many times have you seen a parent or friend try to set up a romance? Was it embarrassing?

4. Why was Julie so worried about Ryan's faith, or the lack of it? Did that make sense to you?

5. If Ryan had not found out how his mother felt about him and his brother, do you think he'd have been able to overcome his hang-ups and forgive himself the way God forgave him?

6. Who could have stolen the time capsule? When and why?

7. Did you worry about Lucy Shaw? Could you understand why a young woman would run

away, particularly in 1926, when women had so few rights compared to today?

8. Julie was actually an internet entrepreneur as well as a rancher. Do you know anyone else like that?

9. Even things that are fun can be a business, like rodeo riding or raising sheep. How many people can you think of who are actually happy to go to work every day? (FYI, I happen to be one of them!)

10. Jasper Gulch is a fictional town, yet true to life in many ways. Do you know of a place like that, where everybody knows just about everyone else and there are minor political and operational spats from time to time?

11. The old bridge was no longer safe for traffic. Can you see why some would want to save it and others resist? Why would they care? Money? Memories? Prejudice against others who disagree?

12. Many older towns lose track of their history as time goes by. Do you think it is something worth preserving?

13. In the end, Ryan adopted Julie's lifestyle, at least in part. Do you think she was wise to tell him he was also free to pursue his rodeo career?

LARGER-PRINT BOOKS!

GET 2 FREE
LARGER-PRINT NOVELS
PLUS 2 FREE
MYSTERY GIFTS

Love Inspired®
SUSPENSE
RIVETING INSPIRATIONAL ROMANCE

Larger-print novels are now available...

YES! Please send me 2 FREE LARGER-PRINT Love Inspired® Suspense novels and my 2 FREE mystery gifts (gifts are worth about $10). After receiving them, if I don't wish to receive any more books, I can return the shipping statement marked "cancel." If I don't cancel, I will receive 4 brand-new novels every month and be billed just $5.24 per book in the U.S. or $5.74 per book in Canada. That's a savings of at least 23% off the cover price. It's quite a bargain! Shipping and handling is just 50¢ per book in the U.S. and 75¢ per book in Canada.* I understand that accepting the 2 free books and gifts places me under no obligation to buy anything. I can always return a shipment and cancel at any time. Even if I never buy another book, the two free books and gifts are mine to keep forever.

110/310 IDN F5CC

Name _____ (PLEASE PRINT) _____

Address _____ Apt. # _____

City _____ State/Prov. _____ Zip/Postal Code _____

Signature (if under 18, a parent or guardian must sign)

Mail to the Harlequin® Reader Service:
IN U.S.A.: P.O. Box 1867, Buffalo, NY 14240-1867
IN CANADA: P.O. Box 609, Fort Erie, Ontario L2A 5X3

**Are you a current subscriber to Love Inspired Suspense books
and want to receive the larger-print edition?
Call 1-800-873-8635 or visit www.ReaderService.com.**

* Terms and prices subject to change without notice. Prices do not include applicable taxes. Sales tax applicable in N.Y. Canadian residents will be charged applicable taxes. Offer not valid in Quebec. This offer is limited to one order per household. Not valid for current subscribers to Love Inspired Suspense larger-print books. All orders subject to credit approval. Credit or debit balances in a customer's account(s) may be offset by any other outstanding balance owed by or to the customer. Please allow 4 to 6 weeks for delivery. Offer available while quantities last.

Your Privacy—The Harlequin® Reader Service is committed to protecting your privacy. Our Privacy Policy is available online at www.ReaderService.com or upon request from the Harlequin Reader Service.

We make a portion of our mailing list available to reputable third parties that offer products we believe may interest you. If you prefer that we not exchange your name with third parties, or if you wish to clarify or modify your communication preferences, please visit us at www.ReaderService.com/consumerschoice or write to us at Harlequin Reader Service Preference Service, P.O. Box 9062, Buffalo, NY 14269. Include your complete name and address.

LISLPDIR13R

Reader Service.com

Manage your account online!

- Review your order history
- Manage your payments
- Update your address

---

*We've designed
the Harlequin® Reader Service
website just for you.*

Enjoy all the features!

- Reader excerpts from any series
- Respond to mailings and special monthly offers
- Discover new series available to you
- Browse the Bonus Bucks catalog
- Share your feedback

Visit us at:

ReaderService.com